UP YOUR CHUFF

Anthony Graves

A Tale of Old Men and the Sea

GROGHAM BOOKS

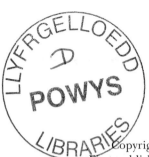

Copyright © Anthony Graves 2011
First published in 2011 by Grogham Books
Glan Yr Afon Barns, Castle Road, Llangynidr, Crickhowell, Powys,
NP8 1NG

Distributed by Gardners Books, 1 Whittle Drive, Eastbourne, East
Sussex, BN23 6QH
Tel: +44(0)1323 521555 | Fax: +44(0)1323 521666

All of the characters in this book are fictitious and any
resemblance to actual people, living or dead, is purely imaginary.

British Library Cataloguing in Publication Data
A catalogue record for this book is available from the British
Library

ISBN 978-0-9566284-0-4

Typeset by Amolibros, Milverton, Somerset
www.amolibros.co.uk
This book production has been managed by Amolibros
Printed and bound by TJI Digital, Padstow, Cornwall

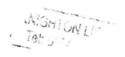

Up Your Chuff

Anthony Graves was born in Kenya in 1948, the son of a War Office civil servant. He was educated at Ifield Grammar School in Sussex and Keble College, Oxford, where he read Modern Languages. After initially embarking on a teaching career in South Wales, he took time out to obtain a postgraduate degree in German Literature from Bristol University. On returning to teaching, he began writing in his spare time, and since retirement has combined this with a long-established love of all things nautical. Following an encounter with a motley crew of like-minded individuals, he has added occasional yachting to his pastimes, and has sailed not only in British and Irish waters but also, more recently, in the Mediterranean and Adriatic. *Up Your Chuff* is the fruit of various experiences undergone over the years with some or all of these larger than life characters.

1

CROATIA – MORNING

"At the third stroke it will be half past eight precisely." In the cabin that he shares with Ivor, Frank is dreaming. He is dreaming of the sleeping clock, on the face of it a theme not calculated to stir passions, but one harbouring nonetheless a peculiar frisson of excitement for Frank. "On the third stroke," the clock is purring, "I shall be defunct...defunct...defunct!" It gives a plaintive moan, then all at once its accents shift from English into Serbo-Croat, a language of which Frank has no inkling. How, his sleeping self briefly wonders, can he be dreaming in a tongue he cannot speak?

This question is destined to remain unanswered. The next instant the dream dissolves in a swirling cacophony of voices and languages before vanishing altogether. He heaves a sigh, mumbles something incoherent and slips into a fitful doze, though were he suddenly to awaken now he would find that in the real world beyond his dreams it isn't half past eight at all but five minutes to seven.

Meanwhile, in the real world – that is to say aboard the yacht *Isabella* at its mooring in Trogir – everything is much as it should be. The boat is throbbing with a curious miscellany of snores. From its aft regions come growls, whines, whistles, murmurs. A splutter, a wheeze, a crescendo of choking snorts swelling to a final cataclysmic blast erupts from the skipper's berth in the saloon. Surely nobody could sleep through that! Yet the skipper does, turning with a snuffle from his back onto his side, deaf to his own volcanic outburst. For a moment the boat falls eerily silent, until a noise like air escaping from a balloon issues from the forepeak where Frank and Ivor are still slumbering. One of them has broken wind. Both grumble in their sleep, shifting sideways on their berths, then all is still again.

From nearby a tuneless church bell starts to toll the hour, and almost immediately a high, insistent bleeping quavers through the yacht. A single mobile phone alarm is bursting into song. As the church bell's echoes fade away another phone joins in, then another. The *Isabella*'s dawn chorus has begun. Greeting the new morning, the mobiles tweet and warble cheerily to each other through the boat. Groans issue from the cabins. One by one the crew awaken, silencing the chirpings as they do so. The skipper is the first to rise. He has little choice. His berth will soon be needed as a breakfast area. Others totter drowsily from their cabins, all with but a single goal in mind.

Thump, thump, thump…! The heads, the boat's two sea toilets, are being flushed. Thump, thump, thump, thump…! All are well aware that the handle must be pumped at least ten times. Any fewer and the consequences could be dire. As every yachtsman knows, sea toilets are devious and temperamental animals with minds entirely of their own. Like horses they must be approached with respect. No one relishes the prospect of having to unblock the heads, least of all at seven in the morning.

The skipper, clad only in his underpants, has already claimed possession of the forward heads. Outside the aft heads door stands Zack, the first mate, in boxer shorts and a tee-shirt emblazoned with the motto 'I don't do mornings!' set above a cartoon image of a dazed and soporific camel. The shirt, a souvenir from Egypt, seems particularly apt. Zack is wearing much the same expression as the camel. The aft heads thump away as Zack hops impatiently from foot to foot, until at last the door opens to disclose the figure of Arthur sporting a string vest, a pair of baggy shorts and ankle length khaki socks. Arthur, old and wise in the ways of the world, is a stickler for decorum. Not for him the underwear in which he has spent the night! He is of a more fastidious bent. His attire lends him a hint of sophistication, a touch of foppish elegance in these surroundings. As he emerges Zack swiftly takes his place, shutting the heads door with a bang.

"Is there anyone in the forward 'eads?" The voice is Stan's. His deep Lancastrian boom resonates through the boat like the wind of a raking cannonball. A staccato popping noise from within gives him his answer. He turns aside to fill the kettle from the galley tap. "Is the gas on?" he thunders to no one in particular.

"I'll see to it, mate," comes Denzil's voice from above. As is his habit in these southern climes, Denzil has spent the night on an airbed in the cockpit. For reasons of his own, he prefers sleeping in the open air, only taking to a berth below when forced to do so by inclement weather.

"I've turned the gas on!" Denzil calls down. For a moment he comes into full view, framed in the rectangle of the companionway. Shorts and tee-shirt alike, he is ablaze with lurid orange. "I'll 'ave coffee if you're makin' tea," he declares, his Devon burr furnishing a light counterpoint to Stan's granite northern bass.

"Seven teas, one coffee!" bellows Stan. "Is everybody 'appy with that?"

There comes a murmur of assent from those around. In the forepeak Frank and Ivor are at last astir. Ivor, grimacing like a malevolent Santa Claus, hugely white and hairy in his Y-fronts, heaves momentarily into view. Scowling at the world in general, he stomps with towel and toilet bag to the forward heads, now vacated by the skipper, and closets himself inside. Following him comes Frank, likewise clad in nothing but his underpants, but just as Frank is about to make a dash for the aft heads he runs foul of George exiting the cramped, twin-bunked side cabin that he shares with Denzil's luggage. Both display the same look of concentrated desperation. Both, however, are doomed to disappointment. These heads too are firmly occupied, and likely to remain so for some while if Zack is running true to form. Reluctantly, with agonised expressions, the two retreat to their respective lairs.

Once in his cabin George shoves aside Denzil's bags, squats on the lower bunk and crosses his legs. At this instant he would dearly love to light up a cigarette. The first fix of the day. At his age, well beyond three score years and ten, his ciggies are a last indulgence, an ultimate enduring passion. But he knows full well that he cannot smoke below deck.

Ivor has forbidden it. Ivor's nostrils can detect the striking of a match upwind a hundred yards away. And Ivor has a fierce aversion to tobacco smoke. George heaves a sigh, picturing in his mind's eye a glowing cigarette, savouring its taste in his imagination, drawing phantom fumes down into his lungs. He coughs instinctively at the thought, though coughing only makes him crave his ciggy all the more.

An elephantine blast of wind resonates from the forward heads. Ivor is about his business.

"What the 'ell be 'e doin' in there, Nisbett?" Denzil yells down from the cockpit. "I should think they could 'ear that in the marina office!"

"Just letting nature take its course!" comes Ivor's voice. "I'll spare you the details for now!"

"Thank Christ for that!" returns Denzil, all too aware of what the details of Ivor's toiletry are likely to entail.

A door bangs open and Zack crosses to his cabin. At last the aft heads are free! Seizing his chance, Frank scurries from the forepeak and hurls himself inside. Such is his haste that no one even sees him. A mere blur of Marks and Spencer's briefs and he is gone!

Arthur, meanwhile, having donned a baggy shirt exactly matching his shorts, is busily loading the saloon table for breakfast. An array of cereals, milk, fruit, marmalade, jam, bread, margarine, juices, cutlery, plates and bowls is gradually accumulated in the table's centre. One by one those members of the crew who have by now toileted and dressed bring their mugs of tea or coffee and place themselves around the fringes of this feast. A prolonged thumping from the forward heads heralds Ivor's re-appearance. He glances appraisingly at the groaning board in passing before stomping on towards the forepeak.

"Christ! Get a load o' that!" exclaims Denzil a moment later, slamming down his coffee mug and leaning out to point in horror at the forepeak doorway, now entirely filled by Ivor's vast and naked rear. Engaged in putting on a fresh pair of Y-fronts, Ivor is bent double in a thus far vain attempt to insert his feet into the leg holes. From the perspective of those at the table, his bared buttocks seem to occupy the boat's whole bow section. Appalled, jaws frozen in mid-bite, they avert their eyes from the sight.

"I'm buggered if I knows 'ow 'e gets that gurt big thing onto that little sea toilet in one go!" observes Denzil with a shudder.

Ivor permits himself a chuckle as he finally persuades feet and Y-fronts to co-operate. "A bit of patience and a sound background in engineering, that's the way to do it when you're my size," he responds, straightening up.

"I presume that's just bulk you're talkin' about, an' nothin' else!" retorts Denzil.

"Well, I'm not one to boast," says Ivor, squeezing his head into a grey tee-shirt.

"There's nothin' to boast about, from what I've seen!" puts in Zack.

"I've had no complaints in that department so far," returns Ivor, bending to retrieve his discarded underpants and toss them onto his bunk. He moves aside to let Frank slip past him into the forepeak before pulling on a pair of shorts. Zipping these up with a flourish, he advances on the table.

"Where's my special margarine?" he demands.

"In the fridge!" booms Stan.

"Pass it over, Arthur, mate."

Along with most of those present, Ivor has his own very particular dietary requirements. No one but Ivor knows the secret of his special margarine, though he predicts the most unsavoury effects for any non-initiate rash enough to try it. Safely quarantined in its plastic box, Arthur passes it to Ivor, who, sitting down and opening the box, proceeds to spread copious quantities of the margarine onto a slice of bread. Others also are now turning to their various medical needs. Little by little the saloon takes on the air of a pharmacist's dispensary. All round the table boxes and packs of pills are produced, their contents precisely counted out, capsules are sorted by colour and size to be grouped in regimented lines, tablets dropped into glasses of water and left to swirl and effervesce away to nothing.

Like antique furniture, this crew has a perceptible patina of age. Not only George but Arthur too is well beyond his biblically allotted span, while all the rest, apart from Zack, have half a century at least of misspent years behind them. As for Zack, he has always been something of an anomaly. The youngster of the crew, a mere thirty-something, he appears out of place among the present company. Yet surprisingly, being so much at odds with his messmates in point of age and fitness does not to seem to trouble him to any great extent. Spooning up the last of his cornflakes, he curiously assesses the outspread medications, wondering with an air of fatalism when the time will come for him to join this band of superannuated pill-pushers.

Frank now re-emerges, more or less fully dressed, deposits himself on the seat next to Ivor, pours a little heap of cereal into a bowl and stares balefully at it.

"How's your head this morning, Ironbladder?" queries Ivor in a superior tone.

"It's been better!" mutters Frank, blanching slightly at this double-edged reference to the resilience of his inner organs.

"On the booze again last night! You never learn!" returns Ivor, a keen glint of satisfaction in his eyes.

Unhappily for Ivor, his diet requires him to abstain from alcohol in any quantity. He looks on those still able to indulge freely in their drink with a frame of mind akin to that of a eunuch in a brothel. Nor is he the sort to accept privation with equanimity. Frank's visible discomfiture this morning imbues him with a heady blend of envy, Schadenfreude and moral superiority, and whilst masticating dutifully on his bread and special margarine he indulges himself in concocting a string of taunts with which to plague his suffering bunkmate for the remainder of the day.

"Before we leave 'ere, skipper," roars Stan from the other side of the table, "I'd just like to nip ashore an' stock up on provisions. If I can find a market, I'll get some fresh fruit an' vegetables. Them as we got last year were bloody marvellous!" On the *Isabella's* muster roll Stan figures as victualler and cook. Food is his consuming passion, and, like several of those present, he boasts a waistline to prove it. "What time were you thinkin' of goin'?" he thunders in the skipper's direction. Even when he has ceased speaking his words tremble on the air like the dying notes of a gong. Frank puts a hand to his aching forehead.

"Not before ten o'clock, I should think," replies the skipper. "There's no rush to be off. This week's cruise is supposed to be a holiday, after all."

"Yes, there's no point in flogging it," states George.

"Certainly not," agrees Ivor, cutting himself another slice of bread. "We're here to take things easy, not to break records."

The rest, including Zack, nod their approval. Ivor is absolutely right. Breaking records is the furthest thought from anybody's mind. As should by now be evident, this is not a crew to go looking for challenges. They have quite enough of these to contend with as things are!

2

DROOL

Well, here we are in Trogir, muses Frank as he stumbles up the steps into the cockpit to gaze across the pontoons of the marina towards the old town on its little island opposite. The sun has already warmed the air, the sky is an unblemished blue, all seems perfect on this early September morning. Trogir, Croatia, a mere ten minutes' minibus ride from Split airport, and a very different world from home The crew had every opportunity to take in this view yesterday, of course, when they came aboard late in the afternoon to await the charter company's routine handover checks. And they sampled at least some of the old town's pleasures later still, dining convivially at a local restaurant in the evening. Some, perhaps, took their sampling rather to excess. At this instant Frank deeply regrets sitting up with Denzil far into the night, imbibing both the balmy Adriatic air and a few drams more of the boat's whisky than was good for him.

From below in the saloon comes a clatter of plates. Good old Arthur at the washing-up as usual. A sudden snatch of wind fans Frank's cheek. He stoops to pick up Denzil's pink plastic airbed from the cockpit seat and slides it down the companionway steps. "I think someone'd better stow this below before the wind takes it!" he calls down.

He hears Ivor chuntering beneath him: "There's that bloody Denzil cluttering up the boat with his junk as usual! Why can't he put his own stuff away?"

An unseen hand removes the airbed from the steps.

"Denzil should consider himself lucky," Ivor can still be heard grumbling, "that no one's let the damn thing down yet."

As Frank goes to sit down, a head appears from the companionway. It belongs to the skipper: "Where is Denzil, by the way?" the skipper asks.

Frank gives a shrug: "No idea! He didn't go off with Stan to get provisions. I saw Stan leaving on his own a while ago."

"Denzil's gone ashore to wash his tackle!" Zack yells from the saloon, availing himself of one of the crew's more colourful expressions for taking a shower.

"Oh, God, he hasn't, has he?" groans the skipper with a dismayed expression. All are aware of the reason for his concern. As a rule it takes Denzil at least an hour to shower when shore facilities are at hand. Just what he gets up to whilst showering no one knows, nor would anybody care to imagine. It is guaranteed that he will return enveloped in a suffocating fog of after-shave, but in all other respects no better groomed or laundered than those of his crewmates who choose to perform their ablutions on the boat. As with everything else he does, Denzil showers in his own time and by his own rules, impervious to the views of others on the matter.

"Ah well," sighs the skipper resignedly, "there's nothing to be done about it now. We're going to have to wait for Stan anyway." His head withdraws and disappears into the saloon. Everybody knows what he is thinking. It is one thing to be reasonably free and easy about departure times, but quite another to have the whole crew kept waiting endlessly for Denzil to sort himself out.

"You all know what he's like," Ivor's voice rises in a schoolmasterly tone from the forepeak hatch. "Someone should have stopped him before he had the chance to get away!"

Casting his thoughts of Denzil from his mind, Frank crosses the cockpit and wanders down the gangplank. Looking to his right, he spots George at the far end of the pontoon, a cigarette dangling from his lips. Old George cuts so spare a figure that, without the cloud of smoke surrounding him, it would be quite difficult to make him out at all. A crewman from a nearby boat, passing too close, inadvertently walks through the drifting haze and breaks into a cough.

"They've made you stand in the corner, have they George?" calls Frank.

"Yes," returns George, gingerly approaching the yacht. "It's Ivor and his sense of smell. Very delicate, you know."

The words are diplomatic, the tone less so. What George says, however, is true. Ivor's nasal sensitivity is unusually acute. This is manifest not only in his powerful objection to tobacco smoke but also in a fierce aversion to the scent of fish, making the most innocent of strolls through fishing harbours especially risky undertakings, and placing restaurants with the faintest fishy taint off limits both for him and anyone accompanying him. His ever more insistent threats to throw up on detecting a mere hint of fish upon the air have more than once provoked a hasty exodus from even the most enticing restaurants by entire crews.

As if to prove George's point, Ivor's voice again swells up from the forepeak hatch: "Is that bloody

Puffing Billy out there polluting the marina? I can smell his fumes from down here! I thought I'd got rid of him! Tell him to clear off!"

The hatch closes with a thump, and George hurriedly retreats to his place of banishment at the end of the pontoon.

"Good morning, excuse please!" a soft female voice falls pleasantly on Frank's left ear. He turns his head to see a vision of dark-haired beauty standing next to him.

"Excuse," repeats the vision in an enchanting tone. "I am Irena. Mr. Bulic from charter office send me. He needs details for form." The vision holds out a clipboard. "Can I come on board?"

"By all means!" responds Frank eagerly, leading the way. As she ascends the gangplank Frank calls for the skipper. Up comes the skipper, his face broadening to an appreciative smile as he eyes fall on the new arrival.

"Please," the vision explains, "Mr. Bulic have need of information, dates of birth of crew for form. You not give them yesterday."

"No, quite right, we didn't," replies the skipper, taking the clipboard and perusing it attentively. Do you need dates of birth for all the crew?"

"Yes," answers the vision with a bewitching smile.

"Okay," says the skipper. "No problem!"

As the skipper reads out their names, the crew,

all of a sudden remarkably keen to be up on deck, provide the missing information. As if drawn by a magnet, George returns, minus cigarette, from his place of banishment, and by sheer luck even Stan makes a reappearance while these proceedings are in hand, laden to the gunwhales with bulging plastic bags, just in time to supply his own details. Despite some mumbling and throat-clearing from the most ancient mariners with regard to years, the task is soon completed to almost everyone's satisfaction.

"One moment please, who is this...this Den-zil?" queries the vision, peering over the skipper's shoulder and noticing a gap in the list. "This one is not here?"

"We think," cuts in Zack, keen to make an impression, "he's gone to wash his...he's gone for a shower."

"He come back soon?"

"That's anyone's guess," Zack replies unhelpfully. "But there's a good chance you'll see him in the marina before we do here. If you see someone dressed like an orange, that'll be him! There's no way you can miss him."

"Orange? Are you sure?" repeats the vision, not wholly convinced.

"Quite sure!" the crew reply with one voice.

"Okay, but if I not see him, I come back."

"Fine!" they all happily agree.

They gaze in fascination as she walks away, hips swaying rhythmically, black hair gleaming in the sun. Zack is starting to slaver.

"Stop drooling, boy! That's my job!" states Ivor.

"Would anyone like a cup of tea?" inquires Arthur with touching innocence. Like most of his compatriots, Arthur holds tea to be a panacea for all occasions.

"Oh, all right," they sigh in unison as they watch the vision gradually disappear, all but Zack feeling deep in their marrow the bitter poignancy of age.

Some time later, their tea consumed or grown cold, those of the crew still loitering in the cockpit hear a familiar voice hailing them. Looking to their left, they see something resembling a bright orange buoy, complete with washing accoutrements, tracing a meandering path towards them through the groups of yachtsmen on the pontoon.

"'Ere lads!" the voice calls out in an oddly high-pitched tone from twenty yards away. "You'll never guess what's just 'appened to I! There I was, just comin' out the showers, mindin' me own business, like, when I 'ears someone callin' 'Denzil!' from behind, an' when I turns round I see this smart lookin' piece wi' a clipboard headin' my way! Nice puppies, I thinks! Nice everythin'!" By this time Denzil has reached the gangplank, but he maintains his breathless narrative even whilst teetering aboard.

"Irena she said 'er name was," he presses on, "an' a right trim little craft she was too! She said as she were after my perticlers, an' I told 'er I'd be more than 'appy to oblige! 'You can take my perticlers down any time you wants to, my lover!' says I!"

Beaming from ear to ear at the thought of the precise particulars he would like to offer the lovely Irena, Denzil is now at the head of the companion-way. "There's only one thing botherin' I," he adds pensively, almost as an afterthought. "I'm buggered if I can work out 'ow she knew who I was! I've never set eyes on 'er before!"

"It must be your distinctive aura," suggests George.

"Distinctive *what?*" retorts Denzil indignantly. "But I've only just 'ad a shower!"

George looks him up and down. Thus attired, is it any wonder Irena had little difficulty recognising him? The words 'Makes I laaff!' plastered in yellow lettering across his shirt front, though doubtless unintelligible to the lovely Irena, serve merely to complete the overall effect.

"Right lads, that's it! I think it's time we were off!" the skipper states briskly, taking command of the situation. So relieved is he to have a full complement back on board that all his previous irritation with Denzil has dissipated. "Let's get that gangplank stowed! Can we have people on the stern lines? Ivor, can you let go the lazy line?"

"Aye, aye, skipper," replies Ivor, making his way forward to the bow while Frank and Stan prepare to cast off astern. At last the crew are starting to feel rather more like proper sailors!

The skipper presses the starting button, stirring the engine into life.

"Ready?" he shouts, taking the wheel.

"Ready!" come the answering calls from bow and stern.

"Let go the lazy line!...Let go stern lines!"

And with the splash of the falling lazy line and the throbbing of the engine the boat moves gently forwards, easing clear of the surrounding yachts, then slowly out into open water. The *Isabella* is under way at last!

3

GAS

They have been chugging along for about half an hour, following the coast to the south-west, when Ivor turns to Frank sitting at his side in the cockpit.

"How's the head now, Ironbladder?"

"Much better, thanks!" A combination of aspirins and fresh air has, it seems, worked wonders.

Ivor takes on a crestfallen appearance. He would rather have Frank's distress last considerably longer. He has put much thought into his catalogue of jibes. "Bastard!" he exclaims, then switches his attention to the more distant figure of Denzil leaning over the pulpit at the *Isabella's* prow.

"With a coat of paint Denzil'd make a hell of a figurehead!" he remarks to no one in particular.

The skipper, still at the wheel, surveys Denzil's

orange outfit. "He wouldn't need any painting. He'd do fine as he is!" he replies.

From his galley below, Stan can be heard rumbling ecstatically over his morning's purchases. "Just look at them peaches! Ripe an' juicy! Bloody marvellous! An' that bread's right tasty too! Melt in yer mouth that does! That'll go down a treat with a spot o' jam. Aye, grand is that!" His head pops up inquiringly from the companionway. "Does anyone fancy some bread? It's a funny colour, a bit yeller-like, but I've just tried a slice an' it's bloody luvly!"

"Oh, all right," says the skipper. "I'll have a slice with marmalade, if you've got any."

"Aye, we've marmalade an' jam, whatever takes yer fancy," roars Stan. "Anyone else?"

It appears everybody wants to sample the bread, including Denzil, and Stan happily withdraws to his galley. Almost at once he is replaced on the steps by George's spare frame. Protruding from under George's arm is something white, shiny and of the rough dimensions of a small dog.

"'Ere, what's the meaning of this?" he demands curtly, addressing this inquiry to Ivor. He offers up the object he is carrying for inspection. It proves not to be a dog at all, but a plastic inflatable sheep complete with long painted eyelashes, seductively half-closed eyes and a salacious smile playing on its rouged lips. "I went to my cabin just now for a cigarette, and this is what I found!" pursues George with more than a hint of indignation. "Some bastard had hidden my pack of ciggys under my mattress and left this on my pillow!"

"Well it wasn't me!" protests Ivor, his face a mask of beatific innocence.

"It wasn't me either!" insists Frank, as George's gaze falls next on him.

Zack says nothing, though the briefest shadow of a smile flitting over his features seems curiously to mirror the sheep's suggestive leer. Unaware of this, George turns and stabs an angry finger at Denzil's back. "I'll lay odds that little bugger had something to do with it! He's always in and out of my cabin shifting my stuff about! It'd be just like him to play a trick like that! I'll have the little sod!"

And having issued this summary verdict, he vanishes below, taking the sheep with him. His cabin door bangs shut.

Ivor, ignoring this brief distraction, now turns his attention to the cockpit instruments. "There's ten knots of wind up our chuff, skipper," he announces. "Shouldn't we be getting a bit of cloth out?"

Perhaps more than anyone else aboard, Ivor is never happier than when indulging in a spot of sail trimming. Few things have more appeal to him than tweaking the boom this way or that, tightening or slackening off the sheets, or consulting the fluttering telltales above his head. All this in pursuit of his ultimate goal: the perfect sail shape. Having applied himself over many years to the subject, he is more than ready to expound lengthily upon its finer points to anyone incautious enough to bring it up in conversation. Needless to say, this crew learned long ago to refrain from doing so.

The skipper glances at the instruments. "Okay," he agrees. "Let's get the sails up while we can."

Needing no further encouragement, Ivor hauls up the foresail, winching tight the sheet, and at the same time dislodging Denzil from his perch. The mainsail quickly following, the engine is switched off and the boat slides smoothly through the waves, heeling a touch to starboard as the wind fills the canvas.

Stan reappears on the saloon steps, a plate piled high with buttered bread and marmalade. "'Ere y'are, lads, these'll 'it the spot! Right crackin' these are!"

Taking the plate from him, Frank offers its contents round. The crew munch contentedly on the bread, concurring wholeheartedly with Stan. The bread, yellowish in colour and slightly sweet, is indeed delicious.

A change of helmsman now, along with a slight change of course. Setting the boat on a more westerly heading, the skipper hands Zack the wheel before sitting down to tuck into his bread. Ivor, meanwhile, temporarily distracted from his sails, is studying the coastline on the starboard side. It slopes away grey and rocky, with scatterings of scrubby trees and shrubs, while a tracery of broken stone walls and long abandoned terraces stretches across the hillsides.

"It must've been the devil's own job scraping a living from this land," he observes. "No wonder the locals gave it up to work in the hotels and restaurants. Farming here'd be a damn sight tougher than waiting on the grockles!"

"Just remember we're the grockles round here," Zack reminds him.

"Quite right," replies Ivor absently, still gazing at the hills. He seems to lapse into a reverie for a while, from which he finally emerges with the assertion: "I was thinking just now of the paps of Jura!"

Long used to Ivor's flights of fancy, the others take this seemingly inconsequential statement in their stride. Like Ivor, they are all familiar with the sensuously rounded hills that, together with the distillery, give the Hebridean island of Jura its main claim to fame. Scanning the coast for any feature that may have conjured up the image in Ivor's mind, none of them can detect anything in this barren landscape to evoke the voluptuous curves of Jura's paps. Nonetheless, Ivor is now well and truly in the grip of fantasy.

"Oh, I do love them paps!" he exclaims in a hoarse rapture of appreciation, his imagination running riot. "Yes, I do!" Having lost all contact with reality, he is working himself up to a frenzy. "I always think," he presses on in the same strained accents, "that if you've seen one pair of paps you want to see..." Panting and struggling to restrain the impulse to froth at the mouth, he breaks off to recover his composure with a deep breath.

"All the rest!" states Denzil, helpfully completing Ivor's sentence.

"No, most of the rest!" Zack corrects him, with the air of a connoisseur.

"Now you come to mention it," interposes Frank in his best pedagogic tone, "I did read somewhere once that Henry VIII always insisted on pert tits and paps!" This information proves too much for poor Ivor. The urge to foam at the mouth is almost irresistible. A whole series of deep breaths is now required to restore him to a state of relative calm.

It is as well for Ivor's state of health that the skipper intervenes at this moment. The skipper, it appears, is at a slight loss on a crucial point of terminology.

"Um...what exactly are paps?" he naively ventures.

This unaccountable lacuna in his knowledge is assiduously filled with a host of graphic descriptions and explanations from every side.

"Ah yes," he at last declares feebly, wishing he had never asked. "I thought that's what they were!"

"If you want my opinion, you lot all need a wet nurse," puts in George from the companionway. The precise point of this remark is lost on everyone but George himself, though the suggestion does rekindle a glint of interest in Ivor's eyes. He is about to take up the idea when his train of thought is unexpectedly derailed by Arthur, whose own mental processes have all the while been moving in a entirely different direction.

"Would anyone like a cup of tea?" he asks.

Down he goes to join Stan in the galley. The latter, still enthusing over his provisions, can be heard growling in tones much like the first stirrings of an earthquake: "Just feast yer eyes on this bacon, Arthur mate, great is that! It'll be bloody grand for lunch with some garlic bruschettas! Slip down like nobody's business, it will!"

After several moments Arthur's head appears from the companionway. "Is the gas on?" he inquires.

The skipper, removing the cover from the gas locker, twists the knob on the gas bottle inside. "It should be on now," he replies.

Arthur disappears again, only to resurface almost

27

immediately. "There's nothing coming through. Are you sure it's turned on?"

The skipper lifts the bottle from the locker and gives it a shake. "It's empty," he announces. "Hang on a minute. I'll swap it for the spare."

He takes out the spare gas bottle. "This feels a bit light," he says with a frown. "I hope for Christ's sake this one isn't empty too! Let's give it a try!"

He connects the spare. Arthur returns below. But for a third time he emerges with a frustrated air. "There's still nothing coming through," he states. "I've a feeling you could be right. Maybe the spare's empty as well."

"Don't tell me those idiots in the marina have let us go out with one empty gas bottle and the other as good as empty!" the skipper explodes.

For some minutes the air in the cockpit assumes a distinctly bluish hue as the crew give fulsome vent to their opinion of Mr. Bulic and his charter company.

"Bugger! Bugger it!" Stan's anguished bellow echoes upwards from the galley. "'Ow the 'ell am I goin' to do me bloody bruschettas now?"

"I'll try Bulic on my mobile, if I can get a signal here," sighs the skipper. "His people have caused this problem. It's up to them to put it right!"

He goes down to the saloon to find his phone. After a short interval of silence the crew hear his voice gradually rising as he conducts increasingly irate negotiations from the chart table. Five minutes later he returns to the cockpit.

"Well, I've explained the situation to friend Bulic with some force," he announces, "and I've managed to impress on him that as we've paid for gas it's his responsibility to get it to us. He's sending a boat out after us. We'll rendezvous with them a bit further along the coast, at the place I've picked for our lunchtime stop. We should be in sight of it quite soon. God knows how long Bulic's people will be, but at least we've not far to go!" He turns to Stan who is hovering in his rear halfway up the companionway: "I'm afraid it'll have to be a cold collation for lunch."

"Right, skipper, I'll 'ave to see what I can rustle up. We can always 'ave the garlic bruschettas tomorrer."

At this Stan and the skipper both return below, the former to his galley, the latter to his chart table. Ivor, meanwhile, having passed the last few moments giving the foresail sheet some timely tweaks, takes from his pocket a small plastic box, slides open its lid and inserts what looks like a yellow tablet into his mouth.

"It's my special sweets," he explains to Frank, who has been watching this procedure with interest. "You'll get the full effect soon. They don't half give me wind!"

"From which end?" asks Denzil anxiously.

"They get me bowels going a treat!" responds Ivor with ominous glee.

Those nearest him shuffle away. George judges this an opportune moment to move to the back of the boat and light up a cigarette.

"Just you make sure you keep your smoke well clear of me, Puffing Billy!" Ivor growls at him.

"My smoke's not that bad," ripostes George. "It's a damn sight better than you releasing wind ad nauseam!"

"I don't release wind ad nauseam," protests Ivor, sucking on his sweet with relish. "I quite enjoy it!"

"That may be all right for you, Nisbett!" complains Denzil. "But no other bugger 'ere does!"

"You've not sampled it yet!" Ivor smiles seraphically at him. He crunches his sweet noisily. The others have an unpleasant sense of deep foreboding.

The skipper pops his head up from below to address Zack at the helm. "Can you see the next headland? Our lunch stop is just the other side of that. Keep the headland to starboard for now, and we'll make our turn as soon as we can."

"Okay, skipper," replies Zack.

Ivor goes back to his tweaking. "This wind'll take us in," he says. "But we'll have to change tack when we turn." As he crosses the cockpit to adjust the main sheet there issues from his hindquarters a blast like a foghorn. Arthur's face, only inches from him, assumes a look of intense disgust.

"Christ, Nisbett! What the 'ell was that?" exclaims Denzil, fanning the air frantically with both hands. "That were a bit quick! What you got in them sweets o' yourn, nitroglycerine?"

"Don't say I didn't warn you!" replies Ivor, prodding nonchalantly at the boom.

From the galley comes an indignant cry followed by a swell of choking coughs. Stan's features, more florid than usual, rise into view. "By God, who were that?" he demands, examining each face in turn. "Were that you, Ivor? Bloody 'ell, we can smell that down there! Good job as we'd no gas burning, or we'd all 've been blown to kingdom come!"

"There's plenty more where that came from," grins Ivor, settling himself back in his seat.

"Why don't you come and stand here in the stern?" calls out George, flicking his cigarette butt into the sea. "You'll give us another ten knots of wind if you can keep that up!"

Disregarding this challenge, Ivor returns his gaze to the coastline. The anchorage for which they are making is drawing close. The skipper comes up, and they prepare to make their turn.

"Right, let's go about now!" says the skipper.

As Zack turns the wheel the boom swings over

and the foresail is hauled smartly onto the other tack.

"Well done, lads!" says the skipper. "We'll head in a bit further under sail, then we'll take the cloth down. This will suit us nicely, I think."

The broad cove they are entering looks very pleasant indeed. Ample space for anchoring, a narrow beach for swimming and shelving rocks on either side, with here and there groups of sunbathers lazing on outspread towels. As the boat enters the lee of the land, the sails are taken in and the engine switched on. Ivor and Frank go forward to the anchor winch, while Zack and the skipper keep an eye on the depth gauge. Twenty metres, fifteen, ten... At last the skipper calls for the anchor to be let go, and the chain clatters noisily down.

"We've got thirty metres of chain out!" yells Ivor after a few moments.

"That should do it!" returns the skipper, easing the boat gently into reverse.

"Has it snagged?" the skipper shouts forward.

There comes a tug on the chain. It tautens, holding the boat's weight.

"Yes, it's snagged!"

"Good! Let's have the engine off!"

The throb of the engine dies away, leaving only the sound of the waves lapping against the hull. Now comes the moment for our heroes' favourite pastime when at anchor: searching the rocks and shoreline for topless females. Denzil has already gone below to fetch the boat's binoculars from the chart table. On re-emerging he scans the beach.

"Strewth! There's a fine pair! You don't get many o' them to the pound!" he yells suddenly. "Crikey! You *are* a big girl! You'll never sink wi' two like that, my lover!"

"Here, let me have a look!" says Zack, snatching the binoculars from him. He sweeps both beach and rocks. "Hmm, I think a closer inspection might be called for here," he concludes, licking his lips. He puts the glasses to his eyes again. "Hmm, yes," he mutters appreciatively. Aware that he is slavering again, he pulls quickly himself together. "Anyone else want a look?"

"Yeah, pass those bins over here!" Ivor takes the binoculars and examines the bay from left to right and back again. "Bloody hell!" he mutters, peering through the lenses. "Look at that old boy with his todger hanging out! What a sight! It's enough to put you off your dinner!"

As if waiting for the word dinner to be uttered, Stan rises into view, passing up plates heaped with enough cold provisions to fill the cockpit table twice over. Cans of beer, fresh from the fridge, are handed round.

"I'm sorry about this," rumbles Stan disconsolately.

"I know it's not much, but it's the best I could do wi'out gas."

"And very appetising it looks, too!" the skipper reassures him.

As for the others, they have no time for talking. Putting aside the binoculars, they launch themselves into the repast.

"Gurt lush this be, me old cocker!" declares Denzil after several minutes, addressing Stan.

"Yes, nice scoff, Stan!" mumbles Ivor, his mouth stuffed with bread, showering a flurry of damp crumbs over Arthur.

"Um, yes, very nice," agrees Arthur, brushing himself down.

"I think I might go for a swim after this, when I've let me grub settle down," grunts Stan between mouthfuls.

"There'll be plenty of time if anyone does want to go swimming," says the skipper.

"What time are we meant to be meetin' this bloke with the gas, then?" asks Denzil.

"Well, half past one was the time we agreed on, but I wouldn't hold your breath," replies the skipper, looking at his watch. "It's gone twelve thirty now. We might have to hang on here for a couple of hours. We'll need to keep a good lookout for him."

The food vanishes before their eyes. Within an amazingly short time nothing is left but breadcrumbs and a few strands of ham fat to feed the fishes. Crumpled beer cans litter the table. Frank is jealously guarding his second, unfinished can.

"Aye, that were all right, that were!" growls Stan, graciously accepting the others' plaudits. "I'll just give me belly ten minutes to settle down, an' then I'm goin' for a dip. Anyone else comin'?"

"Yeah, I'll give it a go," offers Denzil.

"Me too!" puts in Zack. "I've brought my fins. Might as well make use of 'em!"

For safety's sake a large round fender is dropped into the water behind the boat and tied to the rail. One by one the swimmers go below to get changed. Stan is the first to reappear. Padding aft, he lowers himself cautiously down the stern ladder. As his bathing trunks make contact with the surface his face contorts in a grimace of anguish. The water is evidently colder than he was expecting. Steeling himself, he hurls himself backwards in an explosion of spray and thrashes ponderously towards the beach. He is followed by Denzil, entering the water in similar style, and then by Zack, complete with fins and swimming goggles, flopping across the cockpit to perch on the ladder's top step and launch himself with practised ease into the sea. This effortless display is marred only by his sharp cry of shock as he makes contact with the water. Nonetheless, kicking vigorously with his fins, in a few swift strokes he is soon overtaking the labouring Stan.

Those left in the cockpit watch the swimmers' progress. They notice at once that Zack is making for a pair of young women lying bare-breasted on a flattened rock close to the beach. On spotting him scudding predatorily in their direction, the women promptly don their tops. Having reached the shallows Zack stands up, raises his goggles to stare shorewards in feigned admiration of the scenery, then, disappointed, heads off to the cove's far side to see what he can find there. Stan, meanwhile, is still just halfway to the beach.

From the cockpit Ivor is surveying the stretch of water between Stan and the boat. "Where's Denzil gone?" he asks. "He went in after Stan. Can anyone see him?"

All peer out across the *Isabella's* rail. There is no sign of Denzil.

"Nip forward and have a look for him, mate," says Ivor, addressing Frank.

Swilling down the last of his beer, Frank makes his way to the bow. Looking down the anchor chain, he sees Denzil clinging to it, apparently for dear life.

"You all right down there?" Frank calls to him.

"No," responds Denzil plaintively, spitting out a mouthful of seawater. "I ain't! I was just swimmin' along the side when the boat started swingin' an' nearly ran me down! The more I swam away, the closer it got!"

Clearly Denzil is not happy. Ivor, coming forward, throws a fender on a long line to him and tows him along the boat's side to the stern, where he manages to pull himself aboard. The incident has, however, not affected Denzil's habitual volubility.

"I thought I was goin' under!" he explains breathlessly whilst towelling himself dry. "The boat just kept on comin' at me!" Waving his towel in all directions, he demonstrates the frantic motions of his arms in his efforts to escape. "I thought: 'You're a gonner 'ere, mate!' as the old joke goes." He pauses, holding the towel at arm's length. "Well, I says to misself, I can't be doin' wi' this, so I grabs the anchor chain an' 'olds on tight!" He sits down with a look of exhaustion, dropping his towel on the seat beside him. "I reckon I've had enough swimmin' for one day. I'll just 'ave a beer to set misself to rights."

While Denzil goes down to fetch his beer Frank takes up the binoculars. Stan, it appears, has now reached the shore and is basking at the water's edge like a beached whale. Zack, over on the right, has found a rock to use as a vantage point, and is making an exaggerated pretence of ignoring a generously endowed female lying less than ten yards away from him. Frank is struck by the fact that Zack's colouring oddly matches the greyish hue of the rocks around him. After a while Zack evidently loses interest and returns to the water.

Time passes slowly. On the boat the skipper checks his watch. Two-fifteen. He glances towards the cove's entrance. Nothing, not a vessel in sight. He is growing impatient.

"We'll wait another quarter of an hour, and if there's still no sign of Bulic's man we'll go on, gas or no gas. We can't stick around here all day!"

Zack has by this time kicked his way to the boat. Stan too is lumbering back. As soon as he is on deck, Ivor hauls in the stern fender and pulls the ladder up.

"Are we leaving then, skipper?" asks Zack, somewhat surprised.

"We've waited long enough. I'll give him a few minutes more, and if there's still no sign of him by then we'll press on. We can get gas ourselves in the next marina and charge Bulic for it!"

Zack goes down to change. In the cockpit all eyes peer seawards. Still nothing.

"All right, that's it! We're going!" exclaims the skipper, his patience at an end. "Let's have the anchor up!"

Ivor and Frank resume their post at the anchor winch. The engine rumbles back to life, the chain rattles noisily into its locker, the anchor is secured and off they go, out past the headland and into the open sea.

The water has grown distinctly choppier. A swell has risen, rocking the boat as it now makes a turn to the north-west to keep parallel with the coast.

"Sails out, skipper?" asks Ivor eagerly.

But before the skipper can reply, he feels a tap on his shoulder.

"Look behind us!" It is George, facing backwards to shield his newly lighted cigarette from Ivor's view. George is pointing at a yacht coming up astern, its sails billowing in the wind.

"Where did he come from?" asks the skipper.

"I don't know, but it could well be our man," suggests George.

"We'll soon find out!" The skipper eases back the throttle. The *Isabella* wallows gently in the swell. Ivor, having nothing else to do, surreptitiously slips another of his special sweets into his mouth.

All focus on the boat astern. It seems to be making directly for the *Isabella*, and coming up fast. As far as can be made out there is no one but the helmsman aboard. The skipper gives him a tentative wave. The other waves back, brandishing a gas bottle at them.

"It's him all right," says George.

"It certainly is," responds the skipper briskly.

"Right, let's have some fenders out so he can lay alongside!"

There is a flurry of activity as fenders are put out on both sides. By now the other boat has caught them up, and is some fifteen metres to starboard.

Lowering his foresail and switching on his engine, the helmsman hails the *Isabella* across the gap: "I not come alongside. Sea is too rough. You take gas when I go past!"

He turns his boat to cross the *Isabella's* bow.

"He's coming down our port side!" yells the skipper. "Get ready to grab the bottle from him!"

Zack, Frank and Denzil line the side. They watch the boat steadily approach. With one hand on his wheel and the other holding out the gas bottle at arm's length, the helmsman steers as near as he can to the *Isabella's* side. Frank leans forward and makes a grab. Somehow he succeeds in grasping the handle and heaving the bottle inboard.

"I have one bottle more!" shouts the helmsman as he passes by. "Wait, I come again!"

They watch him make a second turn, this time across their stern.

"Very kind of him to bring us two bottles," comments Ivor. "He knows his stuff, I'll give him that! He's doing a bloody good job of handling that boat on his own!"

The boat is now moving towards their starboard

side. Frank, having gone aft, prepares to make a second grab. As the bottle is thrust at him, he lunges out but misses. The gap between the boats is too wide. The other boat slows and falls away a little, opening up the distance even more.

"I throw, you catch!" yells the helmsman to Frank across the gap.

Frank senses a cold rush of apprehension, wondering if he has heard correctly. "Can this bloke be serious?" he mutters under his breath. He watches as the boat drops astern before resuming its approach. He tenses, his pulse quickening. In his mind's eye he sees the bottle landing on his foot or striking him full on the chest. A feeling of disassociation steals through him, as if he is experiencing a particularly bad dream. He pinches himself to check he is awake. All things being equal, any dream, however bad, would be preferable to standing here!

For an instant it looks as if the boat will ram them at the very point where Frank is nervously waiting, but at the last minute the helmsman turns the wheel to swing his cockpit close in towards the *Isabella's* side. With bated breath Frank watches as the helmsman snatches up the second bottle and flings it bodily at him.

To Frank's overwrought perceptions, everything now shifts abruptly into slow motion. He is aware of the bottle floating across the gap between the boats. The nearer its trajectory takes it, the larger it gets. He notices how very like a bomb it looks, and a bomb growing bigger all the time! A phrase echoes dimly in the back of his mind, something about discretion being the better part of valour. Instinctively he takes a step backwards. The bottle is now just a foot from the *Isabella's* side. "It's too low," Frank murmurs aloud. "It won't even reach the rail!" With a weird admixture of dismay and relief, he sees it slam against the nearest fender then ricochet down, straight into the sea.

For Frank time now resumes its normal motion. As for the others, nobody can quite believe what has just occurred. The entire crew stare dumbfounded at the gas bottle bobbing in the waves astern. The skipper is the first to pull himself together.

"Quick, get the boathook! Keep an eye on that bottle! For heaven's sake don't lose sight of it!"

For the next ten minutes the *Isabella* manoeuvres this way and that, circling and quartering, sometimes coming tantalisingly close to its quarry, sometimes missing it by a mile. They try going now backwards, now forwards. They use the boat's bow thrusters to edge sideways. All to no avail! The bottle stubbornly persists in eluding them.

Over the throbbing of the engine they hear a yell.

The other helmsman is hailing them. "I try now!" he shouts. Is that impatience they detect in his voice, or merely his effort to make himself heard?

"He'll never do it on his own!" mutters Denzil.

"You're not wrong there, mate!" Zack agrees.

They watch the helmsman first lower his mainsail then begin to make his approach, gradually edging closer to the gas bottle as if to take it unawares. They see him pass the bottle.

"What did I say? Missed it good and proper!" declares Denzil.

"No!" says Ivor. "He's got upwind of it. He can drift back onto it now!"

As they watch, they see the helmsman gently ease his stern round. His boat begins to move back towards the bottle. Abandoning the wheel, he lies flat on his deck and, to the amazement of the *Isabella's* crew, seizes the bottle by its handle and fishes it smoothly out of the water.

"I not throw! I *give* it to you!" he yells across, going back to his wheel.

On the *Isabella* all hands now line the side. The other boat eases cautiously towards them until the intervening gap is about a metre wide. Again the helmsman holds the bottle at arm's length. When it seems almost within reach Ivor leans out, makes a wild grab for it and misses. Next comes Frank, who adds to his already keen discomfort by missing in his turn. Arthur tries his luck, but losing his balance at the crucial moment topples sideways against Stan, and in a tangle of arms and legs both go sprawling back onto the coachroof. Now only Zack and Denzil are left! As he lunges out, Zack feels his fingers close on empty space. He cries out in surprise, grabs Denzil's shoulder with his other arm, and, thrusting him involuntarily forward, manages to place Denzil's outstretched hand just within clutching distance of the bottle. Gasping at this unexpected propulsion and fumbling for any means of support, Denzil wraps his fingers round the bottle's handle in a vice-like grip. At the same moment he feels Zack hauling him forcibly backwards, and tumbles, his fingers still glued firmly to the bottle, down into the cockpit.

With a dismissive wave and a shrug of his shoulders, the other helmsman, visibly relieved to be quitting the scene, steers his boat clear and heads away.

"Well, if gas bottle hurling counts as a sport round here, you can keep it!" mutters Frank, nursing his wounded pride.

"It's lucky the damn thing only hit a fender and not the boat's side!" says the skipper in an aggrieved tone. "Well, let's at least get one of these bottles connected up, as we've had such trouble getting them aboard!"

"Cup of tea all round?" asks Arthur, limping back towards the cockpit.

An almighty blast, courtesy of Ivor's special sweet, is the sole response.

"I'll take that as a yes," says Arthur as he lowers himself painfully down to the galley and the comforting companionship of his kettle.

4

INFLATABLES

Rogoznica! Rogoznica? How the hell do you pronounce a name like that? The whole crew is having problems with the word, Denzil more than most. Truth to tell, Denzil tends to struggle with unfamiliar names, and this particular specimen has taxed him to the limit. Try as he might, he cannot get beyond the second syllable. But then, anyone who admits to being worsted by the word Hebridean, as does Denzil, cannot with confidence expect Croatian place names to trip lightly off the tongue. After multiple attempts, all fruitless, he has thrown in the towel, contenting himself with the knowledge that he is here, and being here cannot be anywhere else. That will have to do for now.

As may perhaps be surmised, our heroes are at present in the marina at Rogoznica, to the west and a little to the north of Trogir. In the wake of the curious incident of the gas bottle, little of note has occurred during their passage here. Having moored without mishap, showered at leisure, and made hefty inroads into the boat's supplies of gin and whisky before going ashore to dine, the crew last night succumbed at length to sleep in varying stages of inebriation, ranging from Ivor's virtuous near sobriety to the befogged intoxication of Frank and Denzil.

Daybreak finds Denzil stirring in his cockpit bed in a distinctly less than joyous frame of mind. This, it transpires, is neither a consequence of alcoholic dissipation nor of any nightmare wrestling with foreign place names. No, Denzil's present state of dudgeon has been induced by having had to spend the night with nothing but a blow-up sheep for comfort, his airbed having vanished without trace. At this instant he would be hard pressed to say which portion of him is suffering the most, his aching back or his sore neck, severely cricked from balancing all night on his plastic bedmate's slippery belly.

Shifting his body with a groan, he extracts himself from his sleeping bag and peers down into the saloon. Beneath him the unmistakable shape of a semi-naked Ivor looms into view, floating palely towards the aft heads like Moby Dick with a loaded toothbrush.

"'Ere, mate, 'ave you seen me airbed?" Denzil squawks down at him.

Ivor peers upwards, his eyes still bleary with sleep. "No, I haven't," he grunts. "If it's not up there I should think it's still where you put it yesterday."

"I didn't put the bloody thing away yesterday! Some bugger's 'idden it!"

"Well it wasn't me! Now if you don't mind, I've got more important things to do." With which sentiment Ivor drifts on into the heads.

"Bastard!" yells Denzil through the heads hatch as Ivor thrusts it open from below.

He is answered by a sound of escaping wind, but does not wait to ascertain from which end of Ivor it has issued. Muttering evilly to himself, he pads down the companionway in search of clothing. George, fully dressed, moves aside to let him pass.

"Am I right in thinking that's Nisbett decomposing in the heads?" asks George, sniffing at the air with distaste.

"'Ave you seen my airbed?" snaps Denzil, getting straight to the point whilst staring him petulantly in the eye.

"What colour is it?" returns George.

"You bloody well knows what bloody colour it is! It's bloody light red!" bawls Denzil.

"Oh pink! Yes, of course. Now you come to mention it, I did see something pinkish sticking out from under my bunk just now," responds George serenely. "It might've been the corner of an airbed. You'd better go and see for yourself."

"Didn't you 'ear me lookin' for it last night? I went all round both 'eads and the saloon! I came into your cabin twice!"

"No," responds George. "Went out like a light. Didn't hear a thing!"

Scowling, Denzil enters George's cabin. On lifting the mattress what should he espy but his missing airbed, deflated and neatly folded.

"No soddin' wonder I couldn't find it! The old git was sleeping on it all the time!" he mutters to himself. And grimly contemplating schemes of vengeance, he rummages through his bags for something to put on.

Five minutes later he emerges from the cabin feeling a trifle happier with life. Not only has he thought of several unpleasant ways of exacting revenge on George, but he has also donned one of his most prized items of apparel: his Bristol City supporter's shirt. Together with a bright red pair of shorts, this transforms Denzil into a vision in scarlet. His self-confidence restored, he mounts the steps to wash ashore as usual. On coming up to the cockpit, however, he is greeted by an unwelcome sight. A small crowd has gathered on the pontoon, mainly Germans, pointing and staring with undisguised glee at the sheep standing astride his open sleeping bag. The sheep, meanwhile, is insolently returning their gaze, its coquettish leer hinting at a wealth of questionable pleasures. Catching sight of Denzil, the onlookers rapidly disperse, sniggering as they go. Denzil glowers at their retreating backs, then, picking up the sheep, hurls it forcibly into the saloon before continuing on his way.

Down below it takes the skipper several moments to recover from the shock of being struck on the nape of the neck by an inflatable sheep whilst navigating the narrow space between the chart table and his breakfast.

"Will someone put that damn thing away!" he exclaims, indicating the sheep now leering up at him from the floor.

"I'll see to it!" says Zack, picking it up and tossing it into his cabin.

Ivor now appears from the forepeak, where he has attired himself for the day in a grey tee-shirt and enormous shorts. "What's up with Denzil this morning?" he asks.

"He's had a bad night," answers Zack. "Someone hid his airbed."

"Oh, is that all? I'll give him a peck on the cheek later. That'll sort him out," replies Ivor.

"I somehow doubt that," comments the skipper,

like the others grateful that only Denzil has been singled out for this dubious consolation.

Breakfast is attacked with the customary fervour. As its last remains are being finished off and the debris cleared away, Denzil reappears. "Where are we heading for today, skip?" he asks, throwing his wash bag onto an empty seat and only just missing George in the process.

The skipper reaches behind him for his charts. "I thought we could make for Skradin today," he replies. "North of here, up the Krka river. There are waterfalls there that are said to be worth visiting. We can spend tomorrow morning doing that, if everyone's agreed."

"Sounds good to me!" responds Zack.

"Aye, that'll be grand!" rumbles Stan, his head buried deep in the nether regions of the fridge, whose contents he is avidly documenting.

"…be grand!" the fridge echoes back.

"I'll take me camera!" adds Stan, again from inside the fridge.

"…me camera!" quavers the fridge in icy response.

All applaud the skipper's suggestion, all, that is, except George. "You lot go if you like," he states in a somewhat peevish tone. "I think I'll stay on board and give the waterfalls a miss. I've seen waterfalls before, when I was in Australia once, and they were no great shakes!"

The others frown, baffled by this line of reasoning, but say nothing. There is no arguing with George once his mind is made up. With a communal shrug of their shoulders, they turn to more pressing matters, the foremost being the prospect of moving on. Frank, as purser, is dispatched to the marina office to pay the mooring fees, whilst the rest of the crew busy themselves with making the boat ready for departure.

On Frank's return, they slip their moorings and set out into another radiant Croatian morning. The wind has shifted since yesterday, and today's heading puts it dead on their nose. Now they will have to rely on the engine. Disgruntled at having no sail trimming to occupy his time, Ivor goes below to fetch a copy of *The Times* brought from home. Returning to the cockpit, he leafs through it in search of the Soduko puzzles. More a numbers than a letters man, Ivor finds Soduko both a challenge and a means of relaxation. Having located the page, he sets about the most demanding of the puzzles, but after ten frustrating minutes of unproductive calculations he realises he is not on form this morning. Looking up from the paper, he scowls in all directions, then lets his attention stray towards the quick crossword. He scans the clues. At least, he muses, he can cal on assistance from the others should he meet with problems here. After rapidly jotting down a few easy answers, he pauses, his brow knitted in concentration, his pen resting on the page.

"Anonymity: two words, three and four letters, last letter L," he offers up to anyone listening.

There is a lengthy silence. The workings of the crew's combined brains are virtually audible, but still the clue defeats them.

"Are you certain you've got that right?" Frank, at the helm, eventually asks. "I can't think of anything that comes even close!"

"Nor can I!" agrees the skipper.

Ivor studies the page carefully. "Oh!" he confesses shamefacedly. "It's not anonymity! It's animosity!"

"Are you quite sure about that?" asks the skipper.

"Quite sure," returns Ivor, perusing the page again.

"What about ill-will?" suggests Frank.

"Ah yes," says Ivor. "That fits!" He jots down the answer and moves on to the next clue: "African country, eight letters, starting with Z."

"Egypt!" suggests Denzil with more enthusiasm than accuracy.

Ignoring him, Ivor glances round the cockpit.

"How about Zimbabwe?" says the skipper.

Ivor dutifully starts writing out the name. "I did think of that," he says, "but it doesn't seem to fit. Too many letters."

"It should fit. It's got eight letters," puts in Frank. "How are you spelling it?"

"Z-I-M-B-A-R-B-W-E," spells out Ivor. "I make that nine!"

"I think you'll find there's no R in Zimbabwe," observes the skipper.

"Of course there's no effin' R in Zimbabwe, you pillock!" erupts Denzil with abrupt vehemence. "A waste of time this is! If we're gonna do crosswords, we'd do a bloody sight better with someone as can read an' write on the job! An' that means not you, Nisbett, you great dyslectric prat!"

"All right then, you try!" returns Ivor, offering him the paper.

"It's no good givin' it to I! My spellin's no better'n yours!" protests Denzil.

Ivor glances hopefully at Frank, but deciding the latter is unlikely to relinquish the wheel merely to stand in for him as scribe, he folds up the newspaper and lays it on the seat at his side. Growing bored, he stares towards the coast. Still the same hilly landscape with its bleached rocks and grid of broken, abandoned walls. He considers sucking on another of his special sweets, but changes his mind, postponing that pleasure until later. Instead he determines that the time has come to console Denzil for his night's discomfort.

"Come here, my lovely!" he growls, lunging

towards Denzil and puckering his lips in a hideous grimace. "Give us a kiss!"

"Get off, you fat hairy bastard!" yells Denzil, sliding smartly sideways. "You keep that gob away from me! I don't know where it's been!"

Rebuffed, Ivor resumes his study of the coastline. In an inlet on the *Isabella's* beam he spots a small boat lying at anchor.

"Is that a fisherman or a diving boat?" he asks.

"Diving boat, I think," replies Zack, shading his eyes with one hand. "Yeah, they've got a diving flag up."

"Ah, yes, I can see it now," says Ivor, making out the little blue and white swallowtail pennant on the boat's stern. "We've not seen many diving boats in these waters. Too deep d'you think?"

"Maybe," replies the skipper. "But they're in shallow water over there."

They all gaze towards the boat until it ceases to be of further interest. From below they hear Stan rumbling in his galley. Having audited its contents, he is now busily rearranging them in order of priority. The crew find they are starting to feel peckish.

"What's for lunch, Stan?" Zack shouts down.

Stan's face appears in the companionway. "I thought I'd try them garlic bruschettas I were goin' to do yesterday," he roars. "I'll use some o' that yeller bread. Luvly that bread is! Right sweet!" He pauses to lick his lips in appreciation before addressing the skipper: "Are we anchorin' again for lunch, skipper?"

"Yes, I've located a spot on the chart that looks about right. We can drop the anchor and go swimming again, if anyone feels like it."

"'Ow long till we get there?" asks Stan.

"Not long. Three-quarters of an hour at most."

"Right, I'll get crackin' then!" bellows Stan, withdrawing his head below.

Time passes at a leisurely pace. George takes over the helm from Frank, and shortly afterwards an aroma of roasting garlic wafts upwards from the galley. Their noses start to twitch. It is just as well their lunchtime stop is in sight. The anchorage turns out to be a cove like yesterday's, but to the crew's disappointment devoid of sunbathers. Another yacht is lying close to the shore, but otherwise the place appears deserted.

With nothing to distract them, the job of anchoring is soon done. Stan rises from the galley, proudly flourishing his bruschettas to unanimous applause. Behind him comes Arthur, bearing plates heaped with accompaniments of every kind. The crew needs no second invitation to launch themselves ravenously upon this feast, and the ensuing silence is broken only by the sound of eight sets of munching jaws.

"I think," says the skipper after some while, chewing thoughtfully on a plum, "that if anyone does want to go for a dip we'd better get the dinghy into the water. It'll be safer in case of problems." He glances briefly towards Denzil.

"Yeah, why not?" agrees Denzil. "I quite fancy takin' the dinghy for a pootle round the boat, if that's okay with Zack. I can still keep an eye on the swimmers."

Normally, it should be explained, the dinghy falls under Zack's charge. Put any dinghy in the water, and Zack will be at once on the helm. Dinghies tend to bring out the boy racer in Zack, and he derives a childlike pleasure from putting them through their paces, opening the throttle, flipping up the bow, executing the tightest turns, and in the process making as much noise as possible. Now and then his exuberance has been known to get the better of him, as at least one unwary skipper, pitched into the sea in consequence of some such ill-advised manoeuvre, can sadly testify. Today, however, the prospect of playing nursemaid to a bunch of ageing swimmers does not appeal to him, and he is more than willing to let Denzil have his way.

"That's fine by me, mate," he assures Denzil. "I'd rather get the fins out again and go for a swim myself."

Accordingly, once lunch is over and more or less digested, the dinghy is dropped into the water and hauled to the stern. Zack, having donned his flippers, is already ploughing shorewards as Denzil clambers into the dinghy and settles himself inside.

"Pass the outboard down, will you mate!" he calls up to Frank.

Unscrewing the outboard engine from its mounting on the *Isabella's* rail, Frank cautiously hands it down to Denzil, who fixes it in place on the dinghy's transom.

"Don't let go the line for a minute!" he says to Frank. "I just want to check the fuel."

Frank watches as he removes the petrol cap from the outboard's tank and places it next to him on the dinghy's side. "Shouldn't there be a chain to secure that cap?" Frank asks.

"Yeah, there should be, but it's broke," replies Denzil, squinting into the tank.

Just at this moment there comes a ferocious "Hoy!" from close behind Frank's right shoulder. Looking quickly round, he sees George flourishing a pack of cigarettes in one hand and gesticulating wildly with the other.

"Have you been at it again, you little git?" George bawls furiously down at Denzil. "Was it you hid my ciggys in the heads?"

Denzil blinks, his mouth agape. Rarely in his life has he been lost for words, but for one brief moment he is genuinely dumbstruck.

"What the 'ell's got into you, you daft old fart?" he blurts out at last. "I've not been near your bleedin' ciggys!"

"Oh yes you have!" insists George, contradicting him with all the dramatic vigour of an irate pantomime dame. "I've been looking for them everywhere these last twenty minutes! I damn well know it was you! That's twice you've had me now!"

"Eh?" returns Denzil, his voice rising to a falsetto. "I ain't got a clue what you're on about!"

Whilst voicing this denial, he extends both arms outwards in a sign of blank incomprehension. By an unhappy chance, this gesture brings the fingers of his right hand into contact with the petrol cap balanced on the dinghy's side. The cap wobbles, tilts, then plops into the water. Helpless to intervene, Denzil watches it spiral gracefully out of sight.

Once again he is rendered momentarily speechless. Then: "Sh-i-i-t!" he screeches in a tone of high exasperation. "Look what you've made me do now, you stupid old bugger!"

Denzil's cry of distress has drawn the skipper to the stern. He is followed by Stan in his swimming trunks. Briefly Frank tells them what has happened.

"Can we try diving for it?" the skipper asks, glancing at the depth gauge. "We anchored at five metres, but the boat's swung round. We've got eleven metres under us at present," he mutters, a trace of uncertainty in his voice. "Can anyone see Zack? We've no chance of getting to it without him."

They search the cove in all directions. There is not a sign of Zack. Then suddenly Stan roars out: "That's' im there, look! Over by that rock!"

He points to a large boulder on the shoreline. Sure enough, there is Zack with his back to them, in the act of removing his flippers. So perfectly does he blend with the rocks behind him that only his movements give him away.

"Can you grab his attention?" the skipper asks Stan.

"HEY, ZACK!" bellows Stan full into the skipper's ear, with enough force to make the boom rattle. "COME BACK! YOU'RE WANTED 'ERE!"

The skipper rubs his ear. Temporarily deafened, he is aware of Stan, Frank and Denzil gesticulating frenziedly towards Zack. He sees Zack finally wave back in acknowledgement, then stoop to put on his flippers. In no time he is thrashing through the water towards the boat. Reaching the dinghy, he rests one arm on it and stares questioningly up.

"What's wrong?" he inquires.

The nature of the mishap is again explained.

"Right, if someone'll pass me my goggles I'll give it a go!" he states when everyone has had his say. Locating the goggles in a side locker, Stan tosses them down to him. Zack slides them on, takes a deep breath, then plunges forward and kicks hard down towards the sea bed. Peering after him, they watch him move this way and that underneath the dinghy. Finally he comes bobbing to the surface like a cork.

"I can see the cap on the bottom, but I'm not sure I can get at it," he pants. "Just a minute, I'll give it another try."

And gulping in a lungful of air, down he goes again, lashing furiously at the water with his flippers. But again he ascends empty-handed.

"It's no good," he splutters. "I can't reach it! It's a bit too far down!"

Ivor has by now arrived on the scene. "How about tying a bucket to a rope," he suggests. "Zack could drag it along the bottom."

A bucket is duly produced and a rope tied to its handle. It is then passed down to Zack.

"This isn't gonna work!" he reports after a trial attempt. "The bucket's too light. It's floating! We need something to weight it down."

Ivor scratches his head. This is a problem for an engineer. How, he ponders, can the bucket be weighted without the weight either falling out or affecting the bucket's balance when dragged along? He sits down to think the problem out, while advice is heaped on him from all sides.

"What if we cut the bucket lengthways and use it like a shovel?" offers Arthur tentatively.

"We could try making a hole in the bottom and sticking something heavy through it," suggests Frank.

"'Ow about fittin' a length o' chain on it?" says Stan.

"Why not tie Denzil to it? All this is his fault!" mutters George grimly.

While these suggestions are being proffered and rejected, Zack makes one last fruitless effort to reach the cap.

"What we really needs 'ere," states Denzil from the dinghy, gazing into Zack's panting face, "is a diver with the proper gear."

And suddenly, as if magically conjured forth by Denzil's words, what should come throbbing into view but the very dive boat Ivor sighted on their passage here! It is actually entering the cove! They cannot believe their good fortune! Quickly overcoming their incredulity, they begin waving at its occupants, who, looking just a little puzzled, turn and head towards them.

As soon as they are within hailing distance it becomes evident that not one of the newcomers speaks a word of English. Undeterred, Denzil sets about conveying by gesture what has happened. Catching the gist of Denzil's mime, one wet-suited man with greying hair gives a quick nod, picks up a weighted diving belt from the bottom of his boat, fastens it round his waist and then, producing a pair of flippers even larger than Zack's, slips them on and slides over the side. In one mighty kick he is gone. Within seconds his arm breaks the surface, holding the petrol cap aloft like the Lady of the Lake brandishing Excalibur. He passes it to Denzil, who screws it firmly back onto the outboard. The diver holds up a thumb in approval.

"Many thanks!" calls the skipper. "Take these for your trouble!" He holds out a pack of beer cans to the diver, but the latter merely smiles and waves a hand in polite refusal. He hauls himself into his boat, and within seconds he and the boat are making for the far side of the cove amidst a chorus of thanks from the *Isabella's* crew.

Even now, no one can quite believe what has just occurred.

"That were bloody lucky!" grunts Stan, for once roundly understating the case.

"You can say that again!" agrees the skipper. "It must be Denzil's lucky day!"

Denzil is less certain. "I don't think I'll be botherin' with the outboard after all," he announces.

"I'm sure that'll be fine with the rest of us," agrees the skipper.

To everyone's relief the outboard is passed back up and secured safely on the stern rail. George, meanwhile, has slipped below to secrete his cigarettes in a place where hopefully no one but him will ever find them.

The remainder of their time in the cove passes tranquilly enough. Zack resumes his swim, and is joined in the water by Stan. Denzil, unusually subdued, contents himself with floating in the dinghy at the boat's stern. All is as it should be. Nobody is injured, nobody drowned, no one falls overboard, and no damage is done to the dinghy. After a while the swimmers return to the boat, the dinghy is heaved onto the foredeck, the anchor winched up, and they are under way again, on course for Skradin.

There is not too far to go, and soon they find themselves passing between a lighthouse and a stone-built fort at the entrance to a wide river that eventually opens into a broad stretch of water with the town of Sibenik at one end and a tall arched road bridge at the other. Ivor, ever a mine of information, informs them that they are going up a ria, or flooded river valley. The others nod wisely, pretending they knew this all the time. They head on towards the bridge. Passing under it in mid-channel all peer anxiously upwards at the masthead. For one tense moment it looks as if the mast's tip must surely scrape the bottom of the bridge, but they pass through unscathed.

"We must've had a good ten feet to spare there!"

the skipper comments reassuringly, though it must be admitted that even he was looking apprehensive for a while.

Beyond the bridge the water narrows, flowing tightly through a rocky gorge before opening into a broad lake. Crossing this, they re-enter the river proper, its banks now lower on both sides. One more bridge to negotiate, and they are at last within sight of the town of Skradin nestling picturesquely beneath limestone hillsides.

On approaching the shore they are surprised to see a photographer snapping eagerly away at them from a pontoon. As if by instinct, and much in the style of Gilbert and Sullivan's British Tar, the crew set themselves at once to striking manly poses. Their hair may not actually twirl nor their eyes flash, but there is a great deal of pulling in of stomachs, thrusting out of chests, straightening of backs, and assuming of steely expressions. If these actions, strenuous in themselves, do not altogether impede their task of mooring up, they do little to ease it.

Regrettably, there is a limit to the efforts of a group of largely antiquated tars to represent themselves as healthy, fit and virile for very long, even under the most favourable circumstances. If any of our heroes were unaware of this before, they are quickly disabused when, shortly afterwards, the same photographer returns to inveigle them into purchasing the fruit of his labours: a snapshot of boat and crew set within a picture postcard showing disparate views of the locality. The result is sorry proof indeed that the camera does not lie.

'Christ!' every one of them mutters in secret, after examining his portrait. 'Do we really look like that?'

To which the image cruelly responds with a mute affirmative.

Yet all the same, as if to demonstrate that vanity has no limits, they each condescend to buy a copy of the postcard – purely as a memento of the trip of course – before settling down to dispel any lingering regrets for vanished vigour in that age-old recourse of many a British tar: a liberal dose of alcohol.

5

SPHINCTER

Next morning sees Ivor issue from the forward heads with his beard bristling with indignation and an expression dark as thunder.

"Who was the last one to use those heads?" he growls at Zack, Frank and Denzil seated at their breakfast. Ivor's demeanour suggests that of a Grand Inquisitor before a trio of recalcitrant heretics. The three glance uncertainly at each other, wondering what this is all about.

Ivor tries a different approach. "Someone," he enunciates fiercely, "hasn't cleaned the toilet before leaving it. There are stains, suspicious stains, under the seat!"

Beneath the spray of these hissed sibilants the three shuffle uncomfortably. Ivor, fastidious on points of hygiene, shifts his gaze accusingly from one to another.

"Well it weren't I!" mumbles Denzil through a mouthful of cornflakes. "I ain't been near the 'eads. I went ashore to strain the spuds this mornin'."

"So did I," echoes Zack, with a cavalier disregard for the truth.

Frank, unfortunately, is slower on the uptake. As he takes time to think, Ivor edges menacingly forward, overshadowing him with his imposing bulk and jabbing the air in front of him with one finger. "Was it you, then?" he demands, his eyes narrowing to angry slits.

Frank gulps down the piece of bread he is chewing and glassily returns Ivor's stare. He feels like a rabbit caught in headlights.

"I don't know," he begins feebly. "I could've been the last in." He is sensing the onset of panic, but just when all seems lost a faint gleam of recollection dawns. "No…no, wait a minute," he flounders. "Come to think of it, someone did go in after me. It may have been Arthur!" he blurts out, grasping at straws.

His relief is almost tangible. With surprising dexterity Ivor swivels on his heels to confront Arthur, attending in all innocence to his kettle in the galley. Being a little hard of hearing, Arthur is unaware of what is happening. Ivor moves towards him with the lethal resolution of a hungry killer whale.

"Have you been in the heads this morning?" he glowers down at him.

Arthur gives a start. "Uh…what heads?" he asks, blinking.

Ivor's finger strikes outwards to his right. "The forward heads!" he snarls.

"Well, I…um…that is, yes, I did use the heads," stammers Arthur, "but I don't think it was the forward ones. I'm sure it was the aft heads. Yes, I remember now. Ask George. I had to use the aft heads because he got to the forward heads before me!"

"Aha!" mutters Ivor under his breath, rubbing his hands. "A positive lead!" In the excitement of the moment he mentally metamorphoses into Hercule Poirot. His little grey cells are working overtime. He looks towards George, who, facing the companionway and with one foot on the bottom step, is engrossed in tying up his shoelaces.

"Well, was it you?" Ivor growls, prodding George between the shoulderblades.

"Was what me?" replies George, twisting round to confront him with a frown of annoyance.

"Was it you," repeats Ivor, inserting his fingers in an imaginary pair of lapels and pacing the saloon with a decidedly disconcerting mince, "who used the heads last this morning?"

"Which heads?" questions George, unimpressed by Ivor's histrionic antics.

"The forward heads!" Ivor erupts in exasperation.

"How should I know if I was the last to use them?" retorts George. "Anyone could've gone in after me!"

Ivor's countenance is now turning from its usual light pink to an apopleptic red. Planting his left hand on the chart table for support, he wipes the back of his right arm across his brow.

"Well *someone* must've used them last!" he fulminates with a volume that even Stan would struggle to match. Upon which, with an air of impotent rage, he slumps down before the chart table to collect himself.

After several moments he regains a little of his self-possession. "I would be grateful," he states slowly and deliberately, "if *someone* would take the trouble to clean the seat in the forward heads, preferably *whoever* was the last in there!"

Nobody stirs.

Following a silence of some two minutes, Ivor raises himself ponderously from his seat. "All right, if that's the way you want it!" he snarls, stomping his way forward through the saloon. He enters the heads, banging the door shut behind him. The others hear the sounds of squirting liquid, running water and the repeated hammering of the pump. Eventually Ivor re-emerges, a bottle of toilet cleanser in his hand. Advancing on the table, he slams the bottle wordlessly down beside a loaf of yellow bread, then takes a bowl, fills it with cornflakes, splashes milk over the top and with grim solemnity retires to the seclusion of the forepeak. One by one the trio at the table finish their breakfast and remove themselves to the safe distance of the cockpit. Ivor is best avoided for the present.

When, shortly afterwards, Stan returns from his morning shopping, he senses an atmosphere of edginess among the crew. He is aware that George and Denzil have not been on speaking terms since yesterday, but Ivor's glowering taciturnity is wholly unexpected. Inured to such events, however, Stan sets about his everyday routine with his customary energy, sorting through his purchases, placing them in the fridge or on the galley shelves, and voicing his appreciation of the merchandise to anybody who cares to listen.

Arthur hands him a cup of tea, taking another to the skipper at the chart table. In setting it down he accidentally spills some drops onto the tourist information leaflet the skipper is perusing. Shooting a look of disapproval at him, the skipper mops up the offending droplets with a handkerchief. Stan, noting this mute exchange, decides the day is definitely not beginning well.

If nothing else, the minor mishap at least rouses the skipper from his ruminations. He glances at his watch. "I've been doing some checking," he says loudly enough for everyone to hear. "We'll need to take a trip boat from here if we want to see the waterfalls. The boats leave on the half hour. It's five to ten now. If we go soon we can stroll over to the quay in good time for the half past ten boat. Is that okay?"

There are murmurs of approval from all directions, even a low grunt from Ivor in his den. Only George offers no response. Still holding to the principle that one waterfall is much like another, George is determined to stay put. While the rest make ready for the excursion, he climbs up to the cockpit and lights a cigarette.

Within minutes the others are filing down the gangplank. Zack, following Denzil, notices the latter is carrying a haversack. "What's in the bag, mate?" he asks, as they step onto the pontoon.

"Me airbed!" Denzil replies sourly. "I'm not leavin' it on the boat with that old bugger!" He gestures over his shoulder at George expelling a trail of smoke across the cockpit. "Lord knows what e'd do if 'e got 'old of it!"

Letting Zack walk on ahead, Denzil drops back a pace. A flash of puzzlement crosses his face as he mutters to himself: "I dunno what's got into the old fart, or why 'e's so set on 'avin a go at me! Anyone'd think I'd done somethin' to offend 'im!"

Strangely enough, George himself, sucking on his cigarette, is soliloquizing along peculiarly similar lines at this very moment. "I haven't the least idea why that little bastard's got it in for me! What've I ever done to him?" he murmurs through an especially vigorous exhalation of smoke. "Well," he rasps, breaking into a hacking cough, "let him try just one more trick, and we'll see what happens!"

As the shore party leaves the marina, they run the gauntlet of a coven of wrinkled crones exhibiting an assortment of fruit and vegetables on makeshift stalls, and appealing to them in a babble of shrill and unintelligible blandishments to view their wares. For a second Stan seems tempted by a heap of plump figs on a table to his right, but the skipper grabs him by the arm and, before the crones can pounce, hurries him on.

"Don't stop!" the skipper urges. "They won't let you go once they get their hands on you!"

"I just wanted to ask the price!" booms Stan apologetically. "I've not seen any figs I've fancied buyin' yet, an' them uns did look tasty!"

Walking at a brisker pace they pass on, along the town's waterfront to the small quay where the tourist boats tie up. The queue here, they observe, follows the triangular continental style: a wide, amorphous mass at its base narrowing to a tip somewhere up ahead. The sight of this does little to improve Ivor's humour. On joining the queue he at once starts complaining loudly at the quantity of unwashed bodies surrounding him.

"These bloody grockles might try taking a bath from time to time!" he grumbles, his nose twitching furiously.

They shuffle forwards, towards a twin-decked boat that is rapidly filling with sightseers. Will there be space enough for our heroes? Certainly there will! Ivor, shoving his way aboard, elbows flailing sideways, sees to that. Having forced a passage to a metal stairway leading to the upper deck, however, he finds further progress blocked by a buxom female who, bulldozing him aside with her prodigious bosom, proceeds up the steps ahead of him. Ivor glares evilly at her as she pushes past, but to no avail. Only when, halfway up, she strikes her head a ringing blow against a steel crossbeam, does his face brighten. Viewing proceedings with moderately greater relish than before, he cautiously follows her up the steps, spreads himself on an empty seat at the front of the boat and waits for the others to join him.

The boat casts off and heads upriver, under yet another bridge and through thickly wooded scenery extending as far as the eye can see on both sides. The contrast with the bleached coastal landscape is more striking than ever.

"What's this place we're going to called?" asks Arthur, addressing the skipper.

The skipper gestures at the riverbanks. "All this is a National Park. It's named after the river we came up, the Krka." He does his best with the name, though it has, in his opinion, a good deal too many consonants for comfort. He makes a mental note to test Denzil on it later.

"Ah!" says Arthur, his interest waxing visibly. Arthur, it should be explained, is the crew's naturalist, his chief, if fleeting, claim to fame being his unfortunate and misconceived 'discovery' on the Isle of Mull some years ago of a hitherto unknown species of roseate gull. The eventual revelation that he had in fact been duped by a prankster with a herring gull and a can of spray paint left him at the time with a severe case of wounded pride and a permanent and unnatural attachment to kettles. Even now, the memory of the affair rankles with him at odd moments.

Yet like old soldiers, superannuated naturalists never die, and in the great scheme of things such setbacks count for little. Far from being irredeemably scarred by this experience, Arthur is today as eager as ever to investigate any wildlife that might come his way. Ever since leaving Trogir he has been privately lamenting the scarcity of seabirds in the places to which the present cruise has taken him. But this lush river landscape with its wealth of trees and bushes holds more promise. His excitement is mounting by the minute. As the tourist boat pushes on upstream, he eagerly studies the banks with his binoculars for signs of life. He has already noted the odd heron at the river's edge, but he would far prefer to meet with something more out of the ordinary, some form of fauna not before encountered.

The boat slows, heads towards a wooden jetty on the left bank and ties up. Its occupants press together to disembark, Ivor again vociferously bemoaning their travelling companions' lack of personal hygiene. Having fought their way ashore, the group make for a pair of tree-shaded booths to queue for their entrance tickets to the waterfalls. These at length purchased, they amble on along a wooded track and soon find themselves outside a small café fronted by a row of rustic tables. The lure of alcohol proves too much for Frank, who, feigning fatigue, squats down on the nearest bench to scrutinise the drinks menu. The rest inevitably follow suit, all except Arthur, who is not to be distracted even by the prospect of a beer from other, more enticing pursuits.

"I'll press on and have a look round on my own," he says. And, binoculars and camera at the ready, he strides off with determined step.

Half an hour later the others thrust aside their empty glasses and saunter after him. From ahead they can hear a roar of water getting louder all the time, and before long they come within sight of the lower falls flowing foamy white between dark rocks. A handful of bathers are splashing in a roped-off pool near the base of the cascade, while, high above, one man in bathing trunks, bolder than the rest, is perched perilously on a rock promontory overlooking the falls.

"Just look at that feller up there!" booms Stan, his voice competing with the thunder of the water. "Bloody poser! Serve 'im right if 'e fell in!"

"Hey, just a minute! Who's that next to 'im?" exclaims Denzil in astonishment. He points upwards, and the others follow the direction indicated by his outstretched finger. There, inches from the torrent, unmistakable in his baggy shorts, is Arthur, bent in rapt attention over a large stone by the water's edge.

"What the hell does he think he's doing?" splutters the skipper. "Try calling to him to get back on the path!"

Stan does what he can to project his voice across the roar of the falls, but even he cannot penetrate Arthur's fixed air of concentration. An instant later they see Arthur rise, then vanish into the surrounding vegetation.

"Daft bugger!" rumbles Stan.

They go on, up a path cut into the hillside, past stalls displaying little bottles of curiously coloured schnapps which no one appears keen on buying, and after a while arrive at a viewing point looking down upon the torrent.

"Look, there's Arthur again!" shouts Frank, indicating a figure far below them, apparently engrossed in photographing something at his feet.

There is no hope of hailing him from here, even with Stan to hand. Shrugging their shoulders, they proceed up the track. The terrain here is criss-crossed with small streams flowing down into the river. The path meanders over little bridges and along wooden walkways traversing marshy ground. At one bridge Stan glances to his right. There, not a hundred yards away, ankle-deep in the stream and with his back to the bridge is Arthur, his binoculars clamped tightly to his eyes.

"Arthur, get back 'ere!" bawls Stan as if admonishing a naughty child, but Arthur seems blissfully unaware of him. Lowering his binoculars, he splashes off in the opposite direction.

Whilst following the path as it rises and falls or twists to left and right, they catch further brief glimpses of Arthur. At times he is wading through a stream, at others beating a passage through dense undergrowth. On one occasion he is halfway up a tree, on another bounding with goat-like grace across a narrow gap between two rocks.

Increasingly he is attracting the attention of other

tourists. People are pointing him out, following his progress, shouting encouragement, photographing him as though he himself were some rare creature native to the region. A nearby Frenchwoman, having caught him in mid-leap on her camera, is proudly displaying the result to those around her. Each fresh feat is commented upon in a jabber of various languages.

All this is becoming too much for the skipper. "I think we should go back down to the café and wait for him there," he sighs with an embarrassed air

So down they go, staring straight ahead as if defying anyone to associate them with Arthur. At the café they order beers and sit with one eye on the path, looking warily out for any sign of his reappearance.

Just as Frank is weighing up the chances of a second beer, who should heave into view round a bend in the path but the miscreant himself, dirty and dishevelled, his shoes and socks caked in black mud. Despite this unprepossessing aspect, he is grinning from ear to ear.

"Lizards!" he calls out ecstatically. "Dozens of 'em! They're all over the rocks! You should see the pictures I've got!"

He flourishes his camera on coming closer, then settles himself down at Ivor's side. "Any chance of a beer?" he inquires, glancing at the glasses on the table.

For a full fifteen minutes they watch him slowly sip his beer whilst flicking with extravagant enthusiasm through an apparently endless store of photos. Every now and then he holds an image up for Ivor to admire. To Ivor they all look exactly alike, and he makes no secret of this. Ivor is not merely relapsing into his earlier ill-temper, but is fast losing the will to live. His eyes are rolling from side to side as though searching for some avenue of escape. He starts puffing out his cheeks in an agitated manner, but this has no effect on Arthur. In the end, his patience spent, Ivor gets up with a growling harumph and trudges off alone towards the jetty.

One by one the others set off in his tracks. Arthur finally downs his beer and follows them, flicking through his pictures as he goes. The same boat that brought them here is waiting at the jetty, and they make their way aboard and onto the upper deck where Ivor is already seated, sniffing the atmosphere with displeasure. He is still discoursing sourly over the hygiene of his fellow passengers as the boat gets under way and turns to head back to Skradin. When Ivor is at odds with life he does not shy from showing it. His companions leave him to his peevish humour in the hope that a spot of lunch will mollify him somewhat.

Fortunately for everyone, this wish is granted. Ivor does indeed mellow somewhat beneath the influence of his lunchtime bruschettas, and when the time comes for the *Isabella* to slip her moorings after lunch he is more or less his normal self again. They motor down the river through the now familiar scenery of lake, gorge and bridges, and finally emerge from the river into the sea. Here they make for open water before turning to the northwest and the town of Vodice further up the coast. The wind is comfortably on the beam as they come onto their new heading, and before long, with the engine off, Ivor has the sails set and the *Isabella* slicing through the water at a good six knots.

Having spent a while adjusting the sheets, nudging the boom to just the right position and checking that the telltales on the sails are fluttering at a perfect angle, Ivor settles down in the cockpit next to Denzil. Denzil, meanwhile, has produced a brand new pair of dark green croc shoes and is about to try them out. Slipping them on, he stretches forth his legs and places both feet appraisingly on the cockpit table. Ivor prods him with his elbow.

"Look here!" he declares disapprovingly. "I've been running round like a blue-arsed fly for the last five minutes, and there's you with your feet up!"

"I've got things to do too, mate," states Denzil,

twisting his shoes sideways on the table top to judge their effect.

"Get you feet off that table! If my mother could see you doing that, she'd turn in her grave!" asserts Ivor.

"So would mine! The trouble with you, Nisbett, is you're not only a miserable old bastard, you're a nosey old bastard too!" returns Denzil vigorously. "What I does 'as got nothin' to do wi' you!"

"I'm entitled to my say about what happens in this boat. I paid as much for this trip as you did!" asserts Ivor.

"No, you didn't!"

"Yes, I did!"

"No, you didn't!" insists Denzil. "I ain't paid yet!"

Confounded by this unique logic, Ivor adopts a different ploy. Ostentatiously he slips one of his special sweets into his mouth. This has the desired result. Denzil immediately shifts away, his feet sliding from the table. Grinning at his subtle victory, Ivor leans back to gaze out across the water. At present they are passing through a group of islands.

"How far do we still have to run, skipper?" he asks.

The skipper, in the stern, considers for a moment. "It won't be long now," he replies. "At this rate we should be there in forty minutes or so. There's only one thing we'll need to worry about. According to the chart there's a stretch of shallow water just outside this next marina. We'll have to keep a good eye on the depth as we go in."

Rounding the tip of an island on their starboard side, they eventually make out Vodice in a low cleft in the coastline ahead of them.

"Better get the sails in," calls the skipper.

Foresail and mainsail are hauled in, the engine is switched on and the *Isabella* moves forward to its rhythmic throb. As they near the shallows, the skipper, with a look of steady concentration, shifts his gaze repeatedly from the coast in front of him to the *Isabella's* depth gauge. Standing at his side, George helpfully reads out the depth: "Fifteen metres...twelve...eleven...nine..."

The skipper stares ahead. The boat seems dead on course. On the bow they can see Vodice drawing ever closer.

"Seven metres," reads out George. Then in rapid succession: "five...four point five...four...three metres!"

"We're can't be far from the shallowest point," says the skipper in a tone meant to express confidence.

"Two metres!" intones George, his voice quavering in the accents of a vicar delivering his amen.

"We should be just about on the shallows now," says the skipper.

"Point five of a metre!" calls out George with a funereal ring.

The skipper tenses. A droplet of sweat trickles down his cheek. He can feel the blood throbbing in his temples. The whole crew listens, waiting for the ominous crunch of the keel on the sea bed.

"One metre…one point five…two metres!" calls George, his voice rising with relief.

The skipper breathes a sigh.

"Well," says Ivor, slapping him on the shoulder, "that was close! I'll swear I could hear your sphincter contracting just then, skipper! Toot, toot, toot, toot, toot – Frrrt!" Ivor mimics the sound of five shrill bursts of a ship's siren succeeded by a blast of evacuating wind.

The skipper smiles wanly. "Yes," he agrees. "That was pretty close on both counts!"

So saying, he pushes the throttle forwards and they head on towards the town's marina, mooring in uncustomary luxury on an outer pontoon virtually clear of other boats. The evening's gin and tonic will taste all the sweeter for this latest brush with the vicissitudes of command, so the skipper promises himself as, mopping a surviving bead of perspiration from his brow, he thankfully switches off the engine for the last time today.

6

HEADS

If, as the Book of Psalms insists, joy cometh in the morning, then aboard the *Isabella* it unquestionably cometh to some rather earlier than to others. The day following their arrival at Vodice finds certain members of the crew fully occupied at a surprisingly early hour. Stan, the first to rise, has already returned from his shopping, and is delightedly discharging his latest cargo of provisions in the galley. Arthur, in equally contented mood, has for some time been seated at the saloon table poring over the collection of lizard portraits captured yesterday on his camera. Whilst thus engrossed, and between sips from his third cup of tea of the morning, he is absently chanting in a low, singsong voice the words of an ancient Wiltshire ditty learned many years ago at his mother's knee:

"I zeed a sparrer
An' I catched 'e,
But 'e pecked I
So I let 'e went."

On the table before him is a bruised and well-thumbed tome bearing the title 'Flora and Fauna of Continental Europe'. After having closely examined each of his photographs he leafs through the pages of this volume in an attempt to identify its subject.

"Ah, here's a good one!" he murmurs to himself, holding the camera up to the light flooding in from the companionway. "It's very green! I wonder... hmm...yes...if that might perhaps be a Balkan green lizard!"

He flicks through the book until he comes to a picture of a Balkan green lizard, then twists the page round so that the image corresponds most closely to the one in his camera.

"I don't know...it's not easy to be sure..." he muses uncertainly, scratching his head before flicking on to his next snapshot.

From the galley opposite comes a protracted rumble of appreciation as Stan unwraps a slab of cheese and breaks off a small corner to sample.

"By Christ, that's nice!" he exclaims rapturously, smacking his lips. "I'll be 'avin' a bit o' that wi' me lunch! Bloody grand is that!"

"I think this one might be a wall lizard," mutters Arthur from the table, peering intently at his camera. "Yes, the coloration looks about right. Let's see…"

He searches for the relevant page in his book. "Oh, just a minute," he murmurs with an air of puzzlement, examining the pictures on the page minutely. "There's more than one of them!" He reads the Latin names aloud. "Podarcis muralis… podarcis melisellensis…hmm, it's surely got to be either a common wall lizard or a Dalmatian wall lizard!" He scratches at his thinning hair again, turning the book this way and that, and bending his head low to scrutinise each detail.

"These plums look right tasty!" resonates Stan, emptying a bag of purple plums into a plastic box. Unable to resist, he pops one whole into his mouth. "Aye, they are that! Bloody marvellous!" he exclaims, spitting out the stone into the waste bin.

At the table Arthur's head-scratching is becoming audible. His researches thus far have established the existence not only of the common and Dalmatian wall lizards, but also of a third variety classified in his tome as podarcis sicula, or the Italian wall lizard. What is primarily exercising him is that the creature eying him from his camera bears more than a passing resemblance to this last named reptile. Having twisted the page in every direction, even turning it upside-down, the similarity between the two seems indisputable. But this is Croatia, not Italy! His brain begins to whir. Might he, he naively ponders, have chanced upon an escapee from the Adriatic's farther shores? If so, he pursues his train of thought with mounting excitement, could he be on the brink of a significant discovery, a landmark in the natural history of the family lacertidae? He is just starting to speculate on the implications of all this when a vision of the roseate gull sweeps chasteningly before his mind's eye. It puts an abrupt end to all further flights of fancy.

Frowning with renewed uncertainty, he is about to go in search of a magnifying glass on the chart table when Ivor, Y-fronted and toothbrush at the ready, pushes past. Having found the forward heads taken up by Frank, Ivor is en route for the aft heads and his first ablutions of the day.

"Morning!" Ivor grunts to left and right.

"Um…yes…" Arthur responds distractedly.

"M'ning!" mumbles Stan, chewing appreciatively on a slice of ham.

Ivor proceeds on his way. Some minutes later, Arthur and Stan are vaguely aware of the thumping of the heads pump. Though neither pays attention to this sound, what comes next jerks both abruptly from their respective ruminations.

"Aagh! Oh no! Oh…shi..it!" Ivor's cries echo with

piercing intensity through the boat. Almost at once the heads door bursts open and Ivor, as if propelled outwards by some unseen force, comes flying from the doorway, his features contorted in a grimace of mingled horror and disgust. Turning an ashen visage towards Stan and Arthur as they gape at him in astonishment, he points into the heads.

"There's pee all over the floor in there!" he cries in a voice at least an octave higher than normal. "I've been standing in it! And what's worse, it's not mine!"

He clutches at the companionway steps whilst Stan and Arthur warily approach to peer past him through the doorway. Sure enough, the floor inside is coated with a film of yellow liquid, from which a deeply unsavoury scent is seeping into the saloon.

Ivor is now performing some sort of ungainly hornpipe on tiptoe, as if reluctant to place his feet squarely down. Already there is a pattern of damp toeprints where he has been standing.

"It's coming from there!" he moans, indicating an open cabinet set against the right-hand heads wall. Within this cabinet Stan and Arthur can see a largish tank with a small plastic plate on its front. Thin trails of fluid are trickling from the edges of the plate to the floor. "That must be a holding tank!" continues Ivor. "All this started flowing while I was working the pump. When I opened the cabinet the bloody stuff nearly squirted me in the face!"

Drawn by Ivor's lamentations, the skipper pokes his head down from the cockpit. "What's up?" he asks.

Ivor explains the situation once again, omitting no unpleasant detail. Furrowing his brow, the skipper comes down to join the little group. "Mmm," he muses, casting a professional eye into the heads. "Looks like a holding tank."

"That's what I said," replies Ivor, "and it looks like it's full! The toilet pump's over-pressurising it. It should discharge directly into the sea, but unless we can find the control that opens it we've got a problem!"

All glance around the heads, but can detect no sign of any lever or button that might seem to operate the tank. Baffled, the skipper crosses to the instrument panel above the chart table.

"There's a red light on here," he says, pointing to an illuminated bulb. "But I'm buggered if I can see what it's supposed to indicate."

Ivor, abandoning his efforts to stay balanced on his toes, squints at the little bulb. It is certainly lit, but the panel next to it is blank. There is nothing to hint at its purpose.

"I'd guess it's telling us the tank needs emptying," states Ivor authoritatively.

"We already know that! What we don't know is how to do it!" replies the skipper. "Ah well," he sighs, checking his watch. "I suppose this means another phone call to our friend Bulic, assuming he's around this early in the morning!"

Taking his mobile phone, he clambers up to the cockpit, while Ivor, having by now composed himself, leans into the heads to switch on the shower pump. The pump judders into action, slowly flushing the malodorous fluid away. Suppressing a shiver of disgust, Ivor next puts his right foot gingerly into the heads, takes the shower from its hook and, teetering precariously on one leg and with his free hand pressing firmly on the pump button, proceeds to hose down the entire space.

From above the skipper's voice rises in irritation as he remonstrates into his phone. "I can assure you there is one!" he can be heard insisting.

His head appears at the top of the companionway. "Bulic says there's no holding tank on this boat!" he announces.

"Tell him there is, and I've got the proof on my feet!" yells back Ivor, nearly losing his balance.

The skipper claps his phone to his ear. Those below listen as he by turns cajoles, argues, persuades, urges until at last his tone appears to soften a little.

"All right!" they hear him state. "We'll be waiting for them...in about two hours, you say? Fine!"

He calls down the steps: "Bulic is sending some people to check the problem out. It seems he's got contacts in this area. They should be with us in a couple of hours. I've told Bulic that if he doesn't get this sorted he'll have to provide us with another boat. There's no way we're going on from here with a blocked and leaking holding tank!"

"Quite right!" agrees Ivor, hopping out from the heads toilet roll in hand. Having rubbed furiously at his one damp foot with a thick wad of toilet paper, he slams the door shut. "Nobody's to go in there!" he declares. "These heads are off limits!"

With these words he cautiously makes his way to the forward heads, now long vacated by Frank, and locks the door behind him. From the saloon the shower inside can be heard running for a full ten minutes before he finally re-emerges, every inch of him soaped, scrubbed, rinsed and now shining like a new pin. As he disappears into his cabin to dress, the others, joined by Frank and Zack, head for the cockpit to escape the odour that, despite all Ivor's best efforts, is creeping insidiously throughout the boat.

Time drags by. Another long wait for the crew. In due course Denzil, discernible from afar in Bristol City red, comes ambling back from his customary sojourn in the shore facilities to be informed of their predicament. For a while there is some anxiety over

George's whereabouts, in case, unaware of the present crisis, he may have slipped into the aft heads unnoticed. On checking these and finding them to be empty, the skipper dispatches Arthur in search of him. A little later the two return, George assuring the skipper that he had merely absented himself for a quiet stroll around the marina. He too receives the strictest of injunctions to avoid the aft heads at all costs.

After an hour the skipper makes a suggestion. "There's no point in everyone hanging around on the boat twiddling their thumbs," he says. "If we split ourselves up into shifts there's probably time for us all to have a bit of a look round the town. I'll stay on the boat for now if someone's willing to relieve me in half an hour."

"Okay," agrees Ivor. "I wouldn't mind a saunter round." He turns to Frank. "D'you fancy coming along?" he asks.

Frank needs no second invitation. Springing to his feet, he follows Ivor down the gangplank. George too is keen to resume his promenade, and sets off in company with Arthur and Stan. Denzil ventures below to stow his washbag and towel, but is forced to beat a hasty retreat by the unsavoury atmosphere now flooding the saloon. Deciding to stay aboard, he seats himself as comfortably as he can in the cockpit opposite Zack and the skipper, all three keeping a sharp watch for anyone approaching either from the landward side or the open water.

After some forty minutes they glimpse Frank and Ivor making their way back.

"Anything to report?" Ivor calls from the pontoon.

"Nothing yet," the skipper responds, shuffling in his seat.

Ivor can see the skipper is growing restive. "Why don't you take a break?" he suggests as he comes aboard. "We deliberately came back early to relieve you. If anyone does turn up, we can take care of things here."

"All right," says the skipper. "I'll grab a coffee ashore. I won't be long." He glances at Zack. "Do you fancy stretching your legs?" he asks.

"No, I'm okay for now," replies Zack. "I'll wait a bit longer."

"Well, you'd better take this in case they try to contact us," says the skipper, handing him his mobile phone.

"I'll come ashore with 'e," says Denzil, getting to his feet. "I could do with strainin' the spuds again, an' I ain't goin' below to do it!"

Ivor and Frank take the seats vacated by Denzil and the skipper. Thirty minutes more slip slowly by. Ivor, drumming with his fingers on the seat beside him, idly watches a small rib with two occupants putter past. Some moments afterwards, to Zack's surprise, the skipper's phone begins to tweet. He puts it to his ear.

"Yes," he says into the phone, "we're the *Isabella*...the *Is-a-bell-a*...Yes... " His face contorts with concentration. He appears to be having a communication problem. He begins again, emphasising each point as if speaking to a young child: "We're the *Is-a-bell-a*. We're on the *outside pontoon*. There are *only three boats* here! You can find us *easily!*"

He pauses, working out the response, and then: "Right! You come back and look again!"

He removes the phone from his ear. "Arsehole!" he exclaims in an explosion of frustration. "Why the hell can't they send someone who speaks English?"

"Are they on their way?" asks Frank.

"They're here, in the marina! They say they can't find us! They're heading back to look for us now!" replies Zack, his rage slowly subsiding

"They must've been in that rib that went past a minute ago," says Ivor.

"Well if they were, they need their bloody eyes testing!" responds Zack.

Sure enough, a few moments later what should they see puttering towards them but the same rib with its crew of two.

"*Isabella?*" shouts the rib's helmsman.

"Yes!" all three chorus from the cockpit.

The rib turns towards the pontoon. Its occupants tie up and step out. Zack looks them up and down. The first to confront him is a swarthy, grizzled individual with the air of an unnaturally surly Zorba the Greek. The latter's companion is a long, gangly youth with a vacant look. Their appearance inspires little confidence, their demeanour even less.

Most strikingly of all, they seem they have brought no tools with them. Certainly there is not a single tool to be seen in their rib, as the trio on the yacht are quick to note. With a sullen grimace Zorba steps aboard and shakes Zack curtly by the hand. He glares questioningly around. Through a combination of gestures and shouted explanations, Zack does what he can to acquaint him with their plight. Sadly, Zorba's English proves as limited as Zack's Serbo-Croat. Frowning ominously, Zorba descends to the saloon, sniffs the atmosphere, glances into the aft heads, then returns to the cockpit to consult with his companion, who until now has been hovering nervously on the gangplank. The latter blinks dully, communes with himself for a few moments, then turns to Zack and asks in a thick accent: "You khave...khosepipe?"

"Yes, we have a hosepipe" replies Zack with some hesitation, wondering exactly what he wants one for. The boat's only hosepipe is the one employed to fill up with fresh water. With extreme reluctance, he takes it from its locker and gives it to the youth, who hands it on to Zorba.

There ensues what seems to be an animated debate between the pair as to their next course of action. At length, having apparently reached some sort of agreement, they clamber into their rib and manoeuvre it along the *Isabella's* side until they are level with the aft heads. Following further lively discussion and several furtive glances at Zack, who is now observing their progress from the pontoon with growing concern, Zorba tentatively inserts one end of the hose into the nearest outlet in the *Isabella's* hull.

"The silly bugger hasn't got a clue what he's doing!" growls Ivor, descending the gangplank to join Zack. "That's the shower pump discharge he's got there! For Christ's sake tell them the outlet for the heads is below the waterline! The only way they'll get to it is by diving under the boat!"

Zack strives to convey this message to Zorba via the youth. Scowling evilly, Zorba rubs at his stubble, looks from the hose to Zack and from Zack to the hose, resumes his debate with the youth, and then the two haul the rib back to the pontoon. Still scratching his stubble, Zorba comes aboard, shadowed by the youth. They tramp below and vanish into the heads, closing the door behind them.

Sounds of bumping, clattering and scraping rise

from the open hatch above them. The hammering of the pump can be heard, succeeded by a burst of savage cursing. The heads door opens just wide enough for the youth to poke his upper body through the gap.

"You khave…wire?" he calls up the companionway.

On catching this inquiry, Frank, still waiting in the cockpit, communicates it to Zack.

"Haven't they got any bloody thing at all?" exclaims Zack.

Ivor searches through the cockpit lockers for a length of wire. Locating nothing, he sends Frank below to scour the cabins for a wire coathanger. Not one is to be found, so Frank is next sent to the neighbouring boats to inquire if anyone on them might have wire to spare. He returns empty-handed. In the end, harumphing mightily, Ivor stomps off to try his luck at the marina office.

All at once a fierce jabber of raised voices issues from the heads. It seems Zorba and the youth are quarrelling. Fearing violence may erupt at any moment, Zack passes two cans of beer down through the hatch. For a while these have the desired effect. The sounds of argument subside into a low, conspiratorial muttering that persists until the empty cans are handed up, on which the tones of strident discord immediately resume.

Fortunately Zack can now make out Ivor

lumbering back along the pontoon. As he approaches, Ivor holds out a small coil of wire.

"I managed to get this from the boatyard," he states on mounting the gangplank. "It was all they could spare. They did say they wanted anything we didn't use back, though!"

"It's something, at least!!" says Zack, taking the coil from Ivor and passing it through the hatch. "Let's hope it's in a fit state to be returned when these clowns have finished with it!"

Down below everything falls eerily silent. Frank peers through the hatch in an attempt to make out what is going on, but all he can see is the unkempt top of Zorba's head. He decides to shift to the pontoon for a change of scenery. After some moments, gazing at the water, he notices a brownish stain spreading from beneath the *Isabella's* side.

"Hey, look down there!" he shouts excitedly. "I don't know what they've done, but they've cleared something! There's brown stuff coming out!"

From the boat Ivor and Zack stare doubtfully at the stain. It does not strike them as particularly large, nor does it seem to be increasing in size. In fact as they watch, they see it disperse little by little. Anxiously, Zack descends the companionway to find Zorba and the youth on bent knees in the saloon, peering into the open bilges through which a foul-smelling grey-brown sludge is oozing. To his horror

99

Zack realises that, as a crowning achievement, Zorba has flooded the bilges with raw effluent!

Muttering imprecations under his breath, Zack flicks on the bilge pump. It stirs the sludge into motion, sending an even fouler stench through the boat. Zorba, with a vaguely shame-faced air, consults again with the youth.

The youth looks up at Zack. "You khave... sponge?" he inquires.

Swearing more audibly, Zack hunts through the galley for every sponge, absorbent cloth and kitchen roll he can lay his hands on, and gives them to the youth. He calls to Ivor to pass down a bucket, and this too is handed over. Zack notices that neither Zorba nor the youth seem affected by the vile odour filling the saloon. He, on the other hand, is very much aware of it! Overcome by an intense rush of nausea, he climbs hurriedly up to the fresh air.

"Any sign of the skipper?" he asks Frank, after taking in a deep breath.

"I don't think so," replies Frank. He shades his eyes with one hand to scan the marina. "Oh, hang on a minute," he says, "I can see Denzil coming now!"

Sure enough, unmistakable as ever, Denzil can be made out passing a small knot of yachtsmen at the pontoon's landward end. One by one, the figures of Stan, Arthur and George, strung out in a line behind him, become visible. And in their rear, like a mother hen shepherding her chicks, the skipper himself comes into view.

"Thank God for that!" says Zack. "I've about had all I can take of these pillocks!"

As soon as he comes aboard, the skipper is updated on events. Stooping at the companionway, he peers into the saloon to discover for himself what is going on. What greets him is the sight of Zorba and the youth sponging out the bilges by hand and squeezing the foul-smelling contents of their sponges into the bucket. Observing that neither is wearing gloves, the skipper turns from the scene in disgust. By now the whole crew has gathered on the pontoon to watch the water beneath the boat change from a translucent green to muddy grey as the bilge pump does its work. The skipper joins them. Only a shoal of little fish, darting in and out of the spreading cloud, appear to be taking any pleasure in the proceedings.

After ten minutes or so the bilge pump falls silent and Zorba emerges followed by the youth bearing the bucket. Lowering himself into his rib, Zorba plunges both arms into the cloudy water, and paddles them back and forth in a forlorn attempt to wash them clean. Whilst doing so he glowers up at Zack.

"You pay me eight khundred kuna now!" he grunts.

His unexpected command of English takes Zack by surprise, but not for long.

"Eight hundred kuna! A hundred quid! In your dreams, mate!" he retorts.

If he is unfamiliar with this last idiom, Zorba does not show it. His visage darkens to a malevolent scowl.

"You pay eight khundred kuna!" he repeats, and then, his English evidently exhausted, he launches at the youth a flood of Serbo-Croat that judging by its vehemence consists mainly of expletives. At the conclusion of this address the youth turns to Zack. "Boat is clean. You give kuna now," he tells him. "Office in Trogir give money back to you."

"No!" puts in the skipper, interceding between the two. "The *office* must pay you the money! *We* do not pay you!"

The youth conveys this message to Zorba, whose swarthy features now assume a look of menace. He embarks on a further tirade to his companion, but the skipper cuts him short.

"I will phone Mr. Bulic at Trogir," he says to the youth. "I will tell him he must pay you, and I will also tell him that the heads and bilges must be cleaned now with disinfectant. Disinfectant? You understand?"

"Yes, I understand" replies the youth, but he is clearly less than happy with the turn events are taking. As for Zorba, on being told of the skipper's intentions, he sinks into a black sulk from which not even the urgings of the youth can extract him.

Undeterred, the skipper retrieves his phone from Zack and makes his call. After giving a full account of the situation, he presents Mr. Bulic with an ultimatum: either the bilges and aft heads are to be immediately disinfected or the boat must be replaced. The effect of this gentle pressure is to persuade Mr. Bulic that it might be in his interests to speak to Zorba. Reluctantly, given the questionable state of Zorba's hands, the skipper passes him the phone.

There ensues a long and heated exchange between Zorba and Mr. Bulic. Whilst its content can only be guessed at, it apparently concludes with the former acceding with extreme bad grace to the latter's demands. As Zorba thrusts back the skipper's phone he mutters something darkly to the youth.

"You khave things for…khow you say…disinfect?" queries the youth.

This is Ivor's department. Drawing a deep breath, he escorts the two down to the saloon and assembles before them on the table a whole battery of cleansers of every shape and size. He even manages to locate a hidden stash of cleaning cloths and an unused sponge from a corner of a galley cupboard.

Ivar's stomach is beginning to turn as he rejoins his companions on the pontoon and takes position

103

upwind of the *Isabella*. The cleansing process that now gets under way appears to require prodigious quantities of clattering and banging from Zorba and his assistant, though how much of this is mere effect and how much real effort is difficult to know. None of the crew, not even the skipper, can summon sufficient courage to abandon the pontoon and venture below to check on progress. Finally, with one last mighty thud, the pair come up to the cockpit.

"You give eight khundred kuna now!" snarls Zorba, addressing the crew in general.

The skipper's face assumes a shade of red that makes Denzil's outfit seem pale by comparison.

"We will not!" he fulminates. "*We* not pay! *Office* pay!"

Zorba's scowl intensifies. His eyes narrow and his hands ball into fists. He seems on the point of jumping from the boat to assault the skipper. Far from cowed, however, the skipper returns his gaze with icy composure. The two face each other in mute and ominous immobility. This dramatic confrontation looks set to last indefinitely until Ivor decides to make his presence felt. Advancing to the gangplank, he plants one foot on its end, interposing his substantial mass between the pair. Having looked him swiftly up and down, Zorba, overawed, retreats a pace. With a howl of impotent rage, he hurls his sponges to the floor, rushes to the *Isabella's* rail and leaps into his rib. Flinging out a string of maledictions, he starts the engine and casts off. The youth has barely time to scramble in beside him.

With a swish of water they are away, Zorba shaking his fist and shouting hoarsely over the noise of his outboard engine. Even as the rib draws clear, he can be seen kneeling in the stern, gesticulating and yelling furiously towards the pontoon. Loosing a final savage bellow suggestive of a curse on all the crew, their chattels, wives and progeny for evermore, he at last disappears from view, hopefully never to be seen again.

Up the gangplank go the crew, the skipper at their head. Arriving at the companionway, the skipper pauses, sniffs the air, then slowly descends the steps. Peering down behind him, Ivor's face contorts in an expression of distaste as a mingled scent of sewage and disinfectant assails his nostrils.

"This light's still on!" the skipper calls up, glancing at the instrument panel.

"That doesn't surprise me," replies Ivor. "I'd be willing to bet they haven't shifted half the blockage!"

"Well," says the skipper, coming up for air. "At least the smell's a damn sight better than before. It looks as though they've cleaned the worst of the mess in the bilges. We'd best declare the aft heads off limits for the duration." He raises his voice to ensure everyone can hear him. "Only the forward heads to be used from now on!"

There is a murmur of agreement from all around.

"What an arsehole that bloke was!" says Zack, kicking aside the discarded sponge.

"Just be grateful you didn't have to shake his hand!" comments Denzil.

"We'll just have to make the best of a bad job," asserts the skipper. "If we're going to carry on at all it's time we thought about making a move. We've lost half the day already! Let's get that gangplank in. Can we have people on the stern lines and lazy line now, please!"

Taking the wheel, he bends to switch on the engine. They cast off and make their way with some caution across the shallows and out into deeper water. Arthur, harbouring a vague suspicion that Zorba might be lying in ambush somewhere round the corner of an island, keeps a sharp lookout for him as they proceed, but it seems Zorba is well and truly gone. 'Good riddance!' thinks Arthur, and, while the others ogle sunbathers on the shore through the boat's binoculars, he switches his attention to the open sea for any signs of birdlife.

They are again heading northwest, past scatterings of small islets with one larger island on their starboard side.

"What island's that, skipper?" asks Frank.

"Murter," answers the skipper. "We're making for Hramina on the northern end." He checks the speed and the wind direction. "We should be there by about four o'clock at this rate."

Ivor is becoming peckish. It is now well past his lunchtime.

"Anything to eat down below?" he inquires, looking hopefully in Stan's direction.

Stan grimaces. "Aye, there's plenty to eat," he rumbles. "The problem's 'oldin' your breath long enough to get it! I'd need an aqualung down there!"

Ivor subjects him to an entreating stare. "I've got to have something to eat soon! I'll have a funny turn if I don't!" he moans.

Picturing Ivor succumbing to a funny turn, Stan shudders inwardly. He finds the image so deeply unattractive that he gives in. "All right!" he concedes. "But it'll 'ave to be somethin' cold! I'll not be standin' over that cooker makin' bruschettas today!"

"Bring me some food and I'll marry you tomorrow!" says Ivor, puckering his lips threateningly.

The unappealing nature of this offer notwithstanding, Stan goes below to busy himself for some minutes in his galley. Soon plates of bread, cheese, ham and fruit are being handed up. In their wake comes Stan, red-faced and puffing like a steam engine.

"By 'eck!" It gets to you after a while!" he pants. "I've opened the top 'atch, but it'll be better when we can get the side 'uns open as well!"

"When we arrive at Hramina we'll have everything opened up," the skipper assures him. "What's it like down there now?"

"Not quite so bad as earlier on," replies Stan. "The smell's gettin' less bit by bit, but you'd not want to spend long down there!"

"I shall be eternally in your debt, sir!" proclaims Ivor, inserting a slab of ham between two chunks of bread. "If I wasn't so busy I'd give you a kiss now!"

"There's no need for that, I'm sure," growls Stan, seating himself between Denzil and George in the far corner of the cockpit.

"Any beers below?" asks Frank.

The look Stan darts at him leaves Frank in little doubt that if he wants a beer he can get it himself. Easing his way past the cockpit table, Frank inhales deeply, then dives into the saloon. Fumbling in the fridge, he grabs two packs of beer and hurries back up.

"Did you enjoy that?" asks Ivor.

"Can't say I did," replies Frank. "But it was worth it!"

As is to be expected, the beers prove extremely

welcome, and before long a relatively relaxed feeling spreads among the crew.

"We'll all laugh about this later," observes George from the back of the boat, puffing out a plume of cigarette smoke.

"You won't if that smoke gets anywhere near me!" grunts Ivor.

George turns away to blow his smoke over the stern. "It's the skipper I feel sorry for," he says. "He's the one who's got to sleep in the saloon tonight!"

"'E'll be needin' a noseplug, then," growls Stan.

The skipper permits himself a wry smile. "I've known worse!" he says. "I've shared a cabin with Ivor before now!"

Amidst the ensuing laughter Arthur starts collecting the empty plates. Anxious to resume his interrupted studies of the family lacertidae, he is resolved to brave the atmosphere below just long enough to do the washing up and retrieve his camera from his cabin.

"Is there something wrong with his sense of smell?" murmurs Zack as Arthur vanishes down the companionway.

"I reckon there bloody well must be!" booms Stan.

When, after twenty minutes, Arthur still has not returned, Frank goes down to check on him.

"He's all right!" Frank calls up. "He's in his cabin.

You may not believe it, but I think the smell has lessened!"

Everyone is relieved to hear this, the skipper most of all. Little by little the crew settle into their usual routine, alternately watching the shoreline slip by and recalling in appreciative detail the attributes of whichever females have lately caught their fancy.

"Did you lot clock that bird in the restaurant last night, the one sat at the table opposite us?" asks Denzil.

"Which one?" inquires Frank, struggling to remember anything at all of last evening.

"Which one d'you think? The one with the big knockers! I was bloody sorry when 'er stood up!"

"Did you see her headlights, then?" asks Ivor, his interest waxing.

"'Eadlights! I seen 'er sidelights as well!" exclaims Denzil, lost in vivid recollection of the spectacle.

If nothing else, such simple pleasures help to pass the time, and it is not too long before our heroes find themselves rounding the northern tip of Murter Island with Hramina now in sight. Frank proves right about the odour in the saloon. It has become noticeably more bearable during their passage. They moor up with little difficulty, despite a brisk breeze nudging them from the side as they ease the *Isabella's* stern up to the pontoon. With his usual efficiency, Stan conjures up the ritual gin and tonics, and then comes the supreme test: Ivor goes below to sample the air. Though he assumes a pained expression on doing so, he pronounces it more or less breathable.

"It's not too bad up here in the forepeak!" he yells back from his cabin. "But I'm glad I'm not sleeping in the skipper's berth!"

All shower ashore this evening, no one being keen to place unnecessary strain on the forward heads. Later on, a congenial dinner in a town restaurant lifts even the most flagging of spirits, and, just as George has prophesied, they at last begin to see the funnier side of the morning's events.

Returning to the boat replete and variously refreshed, most of the crew go straight to their cabins to settle down for the night, leaving only Frank and Denzil in the cockpit to enjoy their final nightcaps. Whether the skipper is quite as happy as the rest on sliding into bed is not certain, but even he is snoring sonorously enough when, an hour later, Frank, with glazed eyes and unsteady legs, gropes his way through the darkened saloon to pour himself into his berth beside a prone and fiercely wheezing Ivor.

7

SHEEP

All too soon next morning Frank is woken from the weirdest of dreams featuring a boiler-suited Nicole Kidman was shovelling sludge into a cabin strewn with metal coathangers, by the sound of voices drifting through the open door from the saloon. Turning onto his side to listen and ignoring Ivor snuffling in his sleep like an asthmatic hedgehog, he recognises the voices as belonging to Stan and the skipper.

"I'm sorry, skipper," Stan is booming, "but I'm not feelin' too grand this mornin'. I woke up in the night wi' a touch o' wind like nobody's business! Smelt like sulphur, it did! I knew right away somethin' were up! I reckon that squid I 'ad last night might've disagreed wi' me. I've been to the toilets ashore twice already, not wantin' to use the 'eads wi' all the trouble we've been 'avin'. I thought I'd best tell you, so you'd know what was up. I'll just 'ave to try and sleep it off in me cabin."

"Don't worry, Stan," come the skipper's soothing tones. "You get back to bed. It's the only way to deal with it."

"The thing is," thunders Stan, "I'll not be right for doin' any cookin' today, nor for seein' to the shoppin' neither."

"That's no problem," the skipper reassures him. "There are enough of us to attend to that. I'm sure Frank will be able to cope with making lunch. He's quite capable of filling in for one day."

"We need more bread an' milk an'..."

"We'll deal with it, don't you worry!" says the skipper. "You just get back to your cabin!"

"All right then!" Stan resonates. "I'll see 'ow I feel after I've lain down a bit."

All falls quiet after this. Frank settles back in his berth. 'Looks like I'm chef today!' he thinks to himself. Growing conscious of an uncomfortable throbbing in his head, the legacy of his several nightcaps, he reaches for his toilet bag on the shelf at his side and rummages for his aspirins. Locating them, he extracts two from their foil packaging, heaves himself upright, and, sniffing to left and right to check for any lingering odours from yesterday, pads into the saloon to find the skipper rolling up his bedding.

"Stan not well today?" inquires Frank.

"Afraid not," answers the skipper. "Some kind of upset stomach. Probably something he ate last night. Perhaps the two of us could go shopping later to get whatever we need for lunch. It'd help if you could deputise on the catering side, at least for today."

"No problem, skipper," says Frank, filling a tumbler with bottled water and swilling down the aspirins in one draught.

"You all right?" inquires the skipper, glancing at the tumbler.

"Fine! Just a bit of a sore head."

"Aha!" observes the skipper with relief.

Ivor now looms into view. He too savours the air before eyeing the pair suspiciously. "Did someone mention stomach trouble?" he demands, reaching into the forward heads for a bottle of disinfectant spray.

"Stan's not feeling too well. Something he ate, he thinks," says the skipper. "He's lying down in his cabin."

"That's not good news!" grunts Ivor. "The last thing we need now is germs spreading! There's nothing worse than a whole crew going down with gippy bellies! And there's only one toilet between the eight of us!"

So saying, he proceeds to the galley where he sets

about spraying a thick mist of disinfectant over every surface. The handle of Stan's cabin door is subjected to the same treatment. Ivor seems about to turn his attention to Stan himself, dozing fully dressed on his bed, when the skipper, choking in the spreading mist, holds up a hand.

"I think that'll do! There ought to be enough disinfectant swilling round this boat to wipe out all the plagues of Egypt!" he splutters.

"You can never have too much of a good thing!" states Ivor, returning the spray to the heads. On passing Frank he spots the tumbler in his hand.

"Headache, Ironbladder?" he asks hopefully.

"No, just thirsty!" lies Frank.

"Bastard!" Ivor grunts.

"Right," says the skipper, "we may as well get on with breakfast now. After that Frank and I'll see to the victualling and pay the mooring fee. I need to get an updated weather report from the marina office while we're there, if I can."

"Weather turning bad, skipper?" asks Ivor.

"There's a wind getting up. The forecasts so far have been giving strong winds for tomorrow, maybe force seven. We don't want to be out in those conditions any longer than we can help it! We really need to be thinking about where to head for today."

"Are we on the home run now then, skipper?" asks Frank.

"Yes, we'll turn back south today. The boat's got to be back in Trogir by five o'clock tomorrow afternoon. If the forecast is right, we should be aiming to get as close as we can by this evening to save ourselves a heavy run in the morning."

"Where will the wind be from?" asks Ivor.

"From the south-west unfortunately."

"On the nose, then. Definitely not up our chuff!" observes Ivor with a frown.

A noise halfway between a whimper and a snort issues from Stan's cabin. In its tracks comes Stan. He shuffles to the foot of the companionway with an oddly pigeon-toed gait.

"Ooh...!" he groans piteously. "When you've gotta go, you've gotta go!" Easing his feet painstakingly from step to step, he vanishes from view.

Ivor watches him leave, considers spraying the companionway with disinfectant, but, resisting the temptation, takes himself off to the forepeak instead, to return a few moments later dressed in shorts and a grey tee-shirt. Seating himself at the table, he selects a packet of cereal from the locker behind his head.

"Whatever else may bugger you about, there's always breakfast!" he remarks with feeling. "Hey, give that fridge top a good wipe and pass some milk out, will you, mate?"

This request is addressed to Frank, who obligingly

complies. Leaving Ivor to his own devices, Frank now retires to the forepeak to make himself somewhat more presentable. At the chart table, the skipper does the same.

One by one the remaining crew members make their appearance. George emerges first from his broom cupboard, unlit cigarette in hand. Arthur sallies forth next, spruce and sprightly, making for his kettle. Zack meanders from his cabin, rubbing sleep from his eyes. A moment later a pair of orange shorts appears on the companionway steps.

"'Ere!" squawks Denzil's voice. "What's up with Stan? I've just met 'im on me way back from the showers, an' 'e walked straight past! 'E didn't even see I!"

"Stan's got other things on his mind," explains the skipper. "Gippy tummy!"

"Ah, got the runs then, 'as 'e?" replies Denzil. "I thought 'e was walkin' a bit queer-like! 'E put I in mind of a duck wi' a stick up its arse!"

"Harumph!" grunts Ivor from the table, letting this image fade a little before proceeding with his breakfast.

"Well, gentlemen," the skipper addresses them collectively. "I suggest we get ourselves sorted out and leave here as soon as we can. The weather forecast doesn't appear promising. It looks as if we're in for strong southerly winds and lumpy seas, especially tomorrow. Now we're starting on the homeward stretch I'd like to get as far south as possible today. Frank and I have a bit of shopping to do, but that won't take long. If Stan's still held up ashore we'll have to wait for him anyway."

"Right you are, skipper!" says Ivor, prising himself from under the table and handing Arthur his dish and spoon to wash.

Denzil, having descended to the saloon, glances round, his nose twitching. "Strewth! 'Ave you been squirtin' bloody disinfectant round 'ere, Nisbett?" he splutters. "I thought the stench yesterday were bad enough! I can 'ardly breathe in this!"

"At least it's a healthy smell!" retorts Ivor. "You wouldn't thank me if you caught something disagreeable now, would you?"

"I wouldn't want to catch anything you've got!" retorts Denzil, placing his fingers over his nose. "I think I'll 'ave my breakfast in the cockpit, if no one minds. I can't be doin' wi' this first thing in the mornin'!"

So saying, he tips a generous measure of cornflakes into a bowl, splashes these and a good part of the table top with milk, then makes his exit up the steps.

"I think I'll go up too," says Frank. "I'll wait for you up there, skipper. Ready when you are!"

"I'll be with you in a minute!" the skipper replies.

On stepping into the cockpit, Frank looks up at the sky. It is still bright with sunshine, though there are a few more smudges of cloud about than yesterday. A lively wind is tugging at the flags and pennants on the surrounding boats and raising a discordant clanking from the mastheads.

"It does look as if we are in for a bit of a blow," he observes to Denzil who is tucking into his breakfast.

"Yeah, from the wrong direction as well!" responds Denzil between spoonfuls, sliding sideways on his seat to consult the compass. "We'll be needin' the donkey today!" He points with his spoon at the engine switches.

As he goes down the gangplank Frank hears a footstep behind him. He turns to see the skipper. Setting off at a brisk pace the two head for the marina buildings.

Once at the office, Frank goes in to deal with the mooring fee while the skipper stays outside to peruse the weather forecast pinned up in a glass case next to the door. Having gleaned all he can from it, he rubs his chin in a meditative fashion, glancing idly sideways. In doing so he spies Stan issuing from the nearby toilet block and calls out to him. Stan turns to head in his direction. He seems now to walking more normally.

"By 'eck, that were close!" roars Stan from ten

metres away. "I were wonderin' just then what I'd do if I got caught short wi' no cubicle vacant! Bloody good job I found one! I got to it just in time!"

"Feeling any better?" asks the skipper.

"Not really," booms Stan, resting his weight against the wall. "I'm not a 'undred percent! I'll stick to gettin' me 'ead down today, if that's all right wi' you!"

"Do whatever you think best," replies the skipper. "You get yourself back to the boat now! Frank and I will be there as soon as we've got everything we need."

Stan's face falls. "I'm sorry, skipper," he thunders apologetically. "I know it's my job! Let's 'ope I'm right enough to be back in 'arness tomorrer!"

"I'm sure you will be!" returns the skipper. Over Stan's shoulder he spots Frank approaching. "We'll see you back at the boat then, Stan!"

"Okay, skipper!" And off Stan goes, with perhaps the merest hint of stiffness in his stride, leaving Frank and the skipper to continue on their way.

Their errand is soon done. Less than twenty minutes later, they are mounting the *Isabella's* gangplank, each bearing two loaded plastic bags, to be met by Zack, now fully alert.

"The boat's ready for off, skip! We can slip the moorings whenever you want!" Zack announces briskly.

"Right, let's get on with it, then," says the skipper, and without further ado Zack switches on the engine and takes up position at the helm. In the time it takes Frank to pass the shopping down to Arthur in the saloon, the slips are let loose, the lazy line dropped and the boat heads off from the pontoon, leaving Hramina behind.

Out in less sheltered waters the sea is noticeably rougher than before. The boat starts heaving and lurching in the waves. After an interval Stan totters up from his cabin to nestle in a corner of the cockpit. The boat's motions have aggravated his condition. Taking pity on him, the others make space for him to stretch out his legs.

George, meanwhile, in the stern, is having problems lighting his cigarette. He tries bending double, shielding the match with both hands against the wind, but this proves ineffective. He leans over the leeward stern rail, trying to use his body as a windbreak. This also fails, the wind easily circumventing his narrow frame. He tries striking two matches at a time, but with no more success. Frustrated, he comes forward, setting one foot on the top companionway step.

"You're not lighting that bloody thing down there!" snaps Ivor. "The skipper says if he catches anyone smoking below he'll put him in the dinghy and tow him behind the boat!"

The skipper's brow creases at this. He has not the slightest recollection of saying anything of the sort, but refrains from intervening. George, having by this time gone partway down the steps, glares defiantly up at Ivor.

"I'm not smoking below!" he ripostes. "I'm just getting out of the wind to light up!"

With just the back of his head protruding from the companionway, he essays his double match technique again. Happily for him this second attempt proves successful, and with his lighted cigarette clutched between his fingers, he returns to his place in the stern.

Ivor, having spent half a minute harumphing energetically whilst fanning imaginary smoke away, consults his watch. "How long till lunchtime?" he asks, directing this inquiry at Frank.

From the far side of the cockpit comes a heartfelt groan from Stan. Frank checks the time. "It'll be a while yet!" he points out. "It's only half past ten!"

"Suck on one of those sweets of yours if you're hungry!" suggests George. Situated as he is at a distance from Ivor, and more or less secure from the effects of his special sweets, George feels relatively safe in proposing this. The rest take a dimmer view of the suggestion, however, none more so than the hapless Stan.

"Don't you bloody dare, Nisbett!" he rumbles,

coming briefly to life. "I'm feelin' bad enough as it is!"

"Why don't you go below, Ivor, and get yourself an apple?" says Zack. "And while you're there you can get one for me too!"

"A cup of tea would be nice!" pipes up Arthur, for once quite willing to surrender his kettle to someone else.

"Good thinking!" agrees George.

"I'll 'ave coffee!" says Denzil.

"Pass up some biscuits if you're going down," adds the skipper.

Before anyone can add to this barrage of requests, Ivor hastens down to the saloon. Ten minutes later he is handing up mugs of tea and coffee. Finally, an apple clamped between his teeth, a packet of biscuits in one hand and a second apple in the other, he makes his way back up. Seating himself next to Stan's feet, he proceeds to crunch loudly on his apple, while Stan, hiding his face behind his arm, looses another plaintive groan.

The morning wears on, the passage of time marked by routine changes of helm. At half past eleven Ivor is beating a tattoo on his stomach with his forefinger and casting pitful glances at Frank. By a quarter to twelve these glances have grown considerably more insistent. By twelve o'clock Frank can bear it no longer.

"All right!" he concedes, rising to his feet. "I'll make a start on lunch now! I take it we're all happy with garlic bread?"

He goes below, leaving Ivor beaming triumphantly in all directions. Frank quickly discovers, though, that talking of lunch is one thing, but actually getting it is likely to prove an altogether different matter. Here in the saloon every pitch and roll of the boat is accentuated, transforming what ought to be a simple procedure into a formidable challenge. Having set the oven to swing freely with the boat's motion, he plants himself at the table to slice the bread, crush the garlic, and then arrange the whole, liberally dosed with olive oil and garnished with mushrooms and bacon rashers, inside a baking tray ready for roasting in the oven.

Being free to sway at will, however, the oven has now acquired a mind entirely of its own. When, on lighting the gas, Frank attempts to slide his tray into place, the oven front comes swooping sharply downwards, nearly scattering the tray's contents onto the floor. When he subsequently tries to withdraw the tray the oven follows it, and with a sudden upward swing deals it a blow that almost knocks it from his hand. He tries again, with much the same result. A third attempt sees him slither helplessly past the oven as the boat rises on an unseen wave. There now ensues a bitter contest between Frank and the oven, victory going to our would-be chef only when, after suffering several falls and a near knockout, he decides upon a more subtle stratagem. Sneaking up to his opponent on his knees with the aim of taking it unawares, he succeeds in steadying the oven just long enough with his left hand to slot the tray smartly into place with the his right.

Now he can take a breather, and a welcome one at that, for these exertions together with the heaving of the boat have started to make an unsettling impression on his insides. Unsurprisingly, the aroma of raw garlic adhering to his fingers is not helping matters. Clambering up the steps and gulping in a quantity of fresh air, he manages to impose a little calm on his rebellious stomach. Having taken several more deep breaths he descends to resume battle with the oven. As he opens its door to check the progress of the bread, a cloud of garlic flavoured smoke shoots up his nostrils. Sniffing and dabbing at his nose with a sheet of kitchen paper, he turns down the gas and, through watering eyes, attempts to rearrange the bread to ensure an even roasting.

Ignoring the surge of nausea again rising in his belly, he settles on his knees to oversee the cooking process at close range. After some eight or ten minutes in this position, and with cramp setting in, he realises that the boat's lurching motions are becoming less extreme. Struggling painfully to his feet and peering through the galley window, he notes to his relief that they are entering the lee of an island. He hears a thump of footsteps on the deck above, followed by the clanking of the anchor chain. Thank God, they are at their lunchtime anchorage! A last inspection of the tray tells him his ordeal is over. Apart from a few slightly blackened edges, the garlic bread is well browned and ready to be served.

With perfect timing Arthur comes down to assist him, and together they hand up the repast, along with the usual host of accompaniments from the fridge, to their hungry crewmates in the cockpit. As he follows the food up, beer can in hand, Frank sees that Stan has supplanted George in the stern and is staring fixedly at the sea behind the boat. Maintaining this attitude throughout the meal, he cannot be prevailed upon to try even the smallest morsel.

"No, I can't face it!" he rumbles, his head averted. "I'll not be eatin' anythin' today. I'll make up for it tomorrer, don't you worry!"

The others have no great objection to this, there being more for them. As ever, they require less than fifteen minutes to clear their plates. Zack expresses his appreciation of the meal with a resounding belch, the garlic bread is unanimously declared to be almost as good as Stan's, and Denzil proffers the opinion that the entire feast was 'fair 'andsome!'. With all traces of his nausea long forgotten, an air of well-being settling over him, Frank feels obliged to treat himself to another beer while George and Arthur go below to do the washing up.

Lunch over, the skipper, eager to be under way, stirs the crew into life. On goes the engine, up rattles the anchor, and the *Isabella* is on the move again, slipping out from the island's shelter into the buffeting of the wind and waves. Leaving Denzil at the helm, the skipper, still anxious about tomorrow's sea conditions, goes down to listen for a weather forecast on the radio.

Ten minutes later George and Arthur re-emerge from below, George lingering just long enough on the steps to perform another of his two-match tricks beneath Ivor's hostile glare.

"Has the skipper come up with anything on the weather?" asks Zack.

"I think so," replies George through a haze of smoke. "He's listening to it now."

Shortly afterwards the skipper comes up. "I've got the latest forecast," he announces. "It doesn't sound quite so bad now for tomorrow. They're giving winds of force four to five, still from the south-west, I'm afraid. I think what we'd best do now is make straight for Rogoznica. That means about three more hours at this rate. It's a fairish run but it'll give us a good start for Trogir in the morning. We should be fine with that, assuming this forecast is reliable!"

"I'm happy with that, skip!" says Zack, working his way forward past the skipper to get to the companionway. "I'm just going down to strain the spuds!"

And loosing a full-blown burst of wind as a parting shot in Ivor's face, he disappears from view.

"Phuuuh!" gasps Ivor, turning away his head in disgust and fanning furiously at the air around him. "He might have had the decency to hold onto that a bit longer!"

"Now you know what the rest of us have to put up with!" says George, flicking cigarette ash into the sea.

"Oh yes, Puffing Billy, we're all well aware of what *you* have to put up with!" replies Ivor with pointed irony, glancing at George's cigarette.

"So you bloody should, Nisbett!" explodes Denzil, not fully registering Ivor's meaning. "You're the bloody expert!"

A little while after this exchange, the skipper, stretching across Ivor, peers down the companionway into the saloon, a look of concern on his face. "Zack's been a long time in the heads," he says. "I hope he hasn't got the runs as well!" He glances at Stan, who has resumed his prone position on the seat opposite.

"Don't worry about Zack!" Ivor reassures him. "He's got a constitution like an ox!"

"I'll nip down and see if he's okay," offers George, coming forward. "I need more ciggys anyway."

He vanishes below. Almost at once, there rises from the saloon a sharp yell of surprise followed by a clamour of raised voices. In the very next instant something white and oddly ovine in shape comes flying up the companionway, shoots over the recumbent Stan, and, seized by a gust of wind, soars across the boat's port side to settle on the waves some hundred metres astern.

"What the 'ell were that?" cries Denzil, looking back over his shoulder.

"Looked a bit like a sheep to me!" says Frank, mellowed by his two beers.

George resurfaces from below, a pack of cigarettes under his arm and his face considerably more flushed than when last seen.

"Would you credit it! That bastard!" He erupts with a force sufficient to stir even Stan into momentary life. "It was him all the time! I've just caught him red-handed trying to swap that bloody sheep for my ciggys! And I thought I'd put 'em safe from prying hands!"

"Exactly which bastard would that be?" queries Ivor.

"That bastard Zack, who else? He's the only

bugger down there!" rages George. "If I were you," he continues, eyeing Denzil for the first time for days without malice, "I'd get below and make sure that airbed of yours hasn't gone walkabout!"

As he offers this advice, Zack appears behind him, wearing an expression only moderately more sheepish than the sheep itself. He glances round the cockpit. "Where's it gone?" he mumbles.

"Over there!" says Denzil, jerking his thumb backwards.

In perverse imitation of the Good Shepherd, Zack gapes forlornly at the white dot rising and falling in the boat's wake, growing smaller and more distant by the second. He turns to the skipper.

"No chance of a man overboard drill, I suppose!" he suggests hopefully.

The skipper shakes his head. "There's no time for that," he replies. "Besides, I think we're better off without it, don't you?"

Plainly not of the skipper's mind on this point, Zack squats down disconsolately beside Ivor. George, having stowed his precious pack underneath the table top, goes back to his stern seat. His indignation is at such a pitch that he forgets to take a cigarette with him. Denzil, meanwhile, handing over the helm to Frank, vanishes below to check the current whereabouts of his airbed. He returns almost immediately, having found it still safely hidden away.

All the same, he cannot resist subjecting Zack to a suspicious scrutiny on coming up.

This is about as much excitement as the crew can take in one afternoon. Stan, only half-aware of these proceedings, gradually enlivens as time slips by, and shifts from a prone to a sitting position. Lacking much of his old spirit, however, he spends most of the remaining passage contemplating his sandals. In due course George recovers enough presence of mind to light a cigarette, though with every exhalation he still manages to mouth the word 'bastard!' under his breath while darting malevolent glances at Zack.

As for Zack himself, he takes a while to recover from his loss, and every now and then gazes distractedly astern, but the sheep has long since vanished from sight. Denzil, on the other hand, has grown peculiarly vivacious. Resuming his place at the wheel, he treats the crew to several rousing choruses of 'I do love to be beside the seaside', until a growl from Stan and a word from Ivor prompt him to refrain.

It is with some relief that, late in the afternoon, our heroes find themselves heading into Rogoznica and the shelter of its marina. Taking the helm, the skipper coaxes the *Isabella* up to the pontoon, while Denzil, standing next to him with a mooring line, again grapples with the town's name.

"Rogzoz…Rognaziz…Rogiziz…" he essays with mounting frustration. Then, springing onto the pontoon, he turns to the marina attendant looping the lazy line onto Ivor's outheld boathook: "'Oy, mate, ain't there no names round 'ere a normal person can get 'is tongue round?"

Uncomprehending, the attendant shrugs his shoulders.

"There you are!" exclaims Denzil, addressing the skipper. "Even 'e can't say it!"

"I'm sure he can if he puts his mind to it," replies the skipper absently, his attention focused on Ivor and Frank as they work the lazy line forward to the bow cleat.

"That'll do," he announces eventually when all has been made fast. "It's time to break out the gin and tonic, I think."

"Excellent idea!" agrees everyone but Stan, interrupting his meditations on his sandals to grimace at the skipper.

"I might just go for an orange juice, if there's any left, an' it I can 'old it down!" he rumbles manfully.

Before long a more convivial atmosphere descends upon the *Isabella's* cockpit as grievances and resentments evaporate beneath a soothing alcoholic mist. Unsurprisingly this same mist hovers on into the evening, and is still present when, having showered and changed, the crew set off to dine ashore. Even Stan, though spurning all thoughts of strong drink and eating only sparingly, seems affected by it, and is more like his former self when, later on, he plods back with the others to the boat. It is still floating over them as, one by one, they eventually wend their way to bed, and it settles on them like a blanket as, amidst a rising symphony of snores, they drift at last into the embrace of sleep.

8

WIND

Whatever dreams may bein store for them tonight, however, our heroes have less time than usual to savour them. In the small hours of the morning a noise like a passing express train shakes them rudely from their slumbers. A wind, fiercer than the previous night, is sweeping through the marina, making the shrouds hum like piano wires and swinging the mastheads madly to and fro. It tugs and snatches at everything not fixed down, among these being Denzil in his cockpit nest. Blinking and only half-awake, Denzil makes a grab for the upper portion of his sleeping bag which, being unzipped, is rapidly migrating towards his knees.

"Christ!" he exclaims, yanking the bag up to his chin and turning onto his side. "Where the 'ell did this come from?"

He tries to go back to sleep, but the wind, having once claimed his attention, seems reluctant to relinquish it. It launches itself upon him in yet more savage blasts, and the more he clutches at his bedding the more the wind seems bent on wrenching it from him. Having blasted over him for some while in this fashion, the wind next switches its assault to his airbed. He can feel it lifting beneath his legs. Finally, fearful of being swept bodily from the boat, he gives up the unequal struggle.

"Bugger this for a game of soldiers!" he mutters, heaving himself out of the sleeping bag and seizing the airbed before it can fly away. "I've just about 'ad all I can bloody stand!"

Tucking the sleeping bag and airbed tightly under either arm, he slides open the companionway hatch and flings them down into the saloon. Following close behind, he shuts the hatch with a thud and sets about reconstituting his nest on the saloon floor.

"Is that you, Denzil?" the skipper's voice comes drowsily from the darkness.

"Yeah, mate," returns Denzil. "I can't sleep up there. It's gettin' a bit lively!"

He hears the skipper grunt in response. From other parts of the boat come similar sounds. Everyone is fully awake. Not even those who have donned earplugs to mute the others' snoring have managed to slumber undisturbed through this wind.

Denzil settles on the floor and tries to will himself to sleep, but, like the rest, he only managed to doze fitfully.

By slow degrees the light of dawn steals through the boat. As the saloon starts to brighten, Denzil sees the skipper leave his berth and pad past him in the direction of the companionway. He hears the hatch slide open and a renewed howling from the wind. His ears catch the skipper's muttered curse.

"It's blowing a damn hooley up there!" reports the skipper, coming down the steps.

"You're not wrong, mate!" agrees Denzil, propping himself on one elbow. The skipper's face has assumed a brooding look. "We weren't expectin' this much wind, were we?" says Denzil.

"No we bloody weren't!" replies the skipper, pulling on his shorts. "There was nothing like this on the radio forecast yesterday. I'll try to get the latest weather report from the marina office here as soon as I can. The way things are looking," he continues, buttoning up his shirt, "we may not be leaving here today!"

Denzil senses another phone call to Mr Bulic in the offing. "They'll not be too 'appy about that in Trogir," he comments. "The boat's due back this afternoon!"

The skipper needs no reminding. "Yes," he states,

"but if it can't be done it can't be done! I'll not be taking any unnecessary risks!"

"It's your call, skip!" returns Denzil, sliding out from his sleeping bag.

"Would this be a good moment to remind you, skipper," comes Ivor's voice from the forepeak, "that this boat has no life raft or proper life jackets? All we've got are flotation jackets!"

The skipper frowns. What Ivor says is true. There is indeed a lamentable lack of life-preserving equipment aboard. He plainly recalls pointing this out during the inventory check in Trogir. And he can remember the exact response he received at the time: "It is no problem. No bad storms here in Croatia! Law says no need of life raft. If you need raft, you must use dinghy!"

Even then the thought of eight large men crammed into one small inflatable dinghy had not been appealing. Now, in recollection, these words take on a distinctly hollow ring. The skipper's expression grows darker still.

"Yes, I'm fully aware of that," he calls back to Ivor. "Everything depends on today's weather forecast. I'm making no decisions until I know what's happening out there!" He waves an arm in the general direction of the open sea. "And as we can't find out anything before the office opens, we'll just have to sit tight."

In varying states of dress, the crew gather round the saloon table for breakfast. In addition to their usual morning medications the more cautious among them, Stan in particular, are taking out their seasickness tablets to wash down with Arthur's tea. Under these circumstances they are not taking any chances.

After breakfast, with a creeping sense of fatalism, the skipper and Frank set out for the marina office. When they return, half an hour later, the skipper's features appear more sombre than ever.

"The news isn't good," he announces on coming aboard. Today's forecast is giving fifty knot winds. I don't see how we can even consider putting to sea in conditions like that. If you ask me, our best plan would be to leave the boat here and get back to Trogir with our gear by taxi. It's not that far, only fifteen miles or so overland. We'll need the charter company's say-so, of course"

"Well, you'd better contact friend Bulic again and see what he's got to say about that," says Ivor. "But I'll lay odds he won't like the idea."

"Well, I'll give it a go," sighs the skipper,

Phone in hand, up to the cockpit he goes. After several abortive attempts, he succeeds eventually in making contact with Mr. Bulic. In the saloon the crew strain to catch the drift of the conversation through the howling wind. What they hear does not augur well. Though the skipper argues the case for leaving the boat in Rogoznica with consummate eloquence, he is clearly making little headway. Mr. Bulic is not to be persuaded.

In the end they hear the skipper reluctantly agree: "Yes…yes, all right then, if you insist we'll have to give it a try. What's that? There'll be someone at the fuel pontoon to meet us? Right, we'll look out for him."

He clumps down the steps. "It's like talking to a brick wall!" he declares angrily. "Bulic won't countenance the idea of leaving the boat here. He says that if we do we'll have to pay an additional charge, and it's likely to be substantial! It seems, gentlemen, there's not much choice. We've got a rough passage ahead of us!"

The skipper's sombre look is catching. It spreads throughout the crew. One or two are blanching visibly at the thought of having to pay an indemnity. Those who have not yet swallowed seasickness pills now hurry off to find some. The skipper gives Stan an appraising glance.

"Will you be okay?" he asks.

"Aye," responds Stan phlegmatically. "I'll be all right. I'm not feelin' bad now. I knew it wouldn't last more than a day."

The skipper nods approvingly, then goes forward to watch Ivor breaking out the boat's stock of flotation jackets and harnesses from the locker under the forepeak berths. Ivor comments disparagingly on the jackets as he passes them to Frank standing behind him.

"Look at these!" he grumbles. "They could at least have given us something decent! And not even a life raft either! If we get into trouble, it's just these and the dinghy!"

"And there's no way we're all gonna fit into that!" calls Denzil from George's cabin. "Certainly not wi' you and your big fat arse, Nisbett!"

"You leave my arse out of this!" responds Ivor, managing a chuckle despite everything. "It's not your concern!"

"It bloody well will be if it takes up my place in the dinghy, you gurt big lump!" retorts Denzil indignantly.

"I agree our situation isn't ideal," puts in the skipper, interrupting this friendly banter, "But we'll have to make do with what we've got. Just see that everyone gets a jacket and a harness. If it does get really bad out there, at least we'll be able to clip onto the boat."

In due course all is ready for departure. As a last precaution the skipper has the cockpit bimini lowered to prevent it being damaged by the wind.

"Let's 'ope it don't rain now!" remarks Denzil as he helps Zack fold the canopy down onto the stern.

On goes the engine, down plops the lazy line, the stern lines are hauled in, and the *Isabella* chugs slowly out to face the worst the weather has to offer. Having scoured their luggage for every scrap of waterproof clothing they can find, the crew huddle in the cockpit. No one has the least wish to go below where every motion of the boat is exaggerated.

Soon the *Isabella's* bow is rearing onto each new wave-crest and plunging heavily down into the next trough. From time to time the hull judders hard against a wave, sending a cascade of spray whipping back across the cockpit. Denzil, at the wheel, huddles low in a vain attempt to avoid these showers. On either side of him sit Ivor and the skipper. Like the tamed wise monkeys, the three raise their hands in unison to shield their faces from the spray, but despite their efforts they are getting more thoroughly drenched by the minute. Denzil tries to raise his spirits with a song, but even his rendition of 'I do love to be beside the seaside' falters after the opening lines.

At the forward end of the cockpit, Stan, on the other hand, is peculiarly cheerful. Despite being incongruously attired in a purple anorak belonging to his wife, he looks for all the world wholly recovered from his indisposition. As the boat lurches into yet another trough, he beams blithely at Arthur sitting opposite, hunched in a showerproof hooded jacket.

141

"I were thinkin' just now o' that fart I did the night before last!" Stan bellows above the noise of the wind and the sea. "By God, you should've smelt it! A bit like rotten eggs it were, only worse! Even Ivor's special sweets could never 'ave bred one like that."

Arthur smiles feebly back. Still waiting for his seasickness tablets to take effect, he is in no humour for such subjects. Shuffling his legs, he leans back to take a breath of air, but as the wind snatches at his hood he receives instead a slap of spray full on the side of his face. With an anguished expression he bends forward to gaze down at his shoes.

George, meanwhile, is contemplating lighting up a ciggy. It seems a challenge, but being on Stan's side of the cockpit he is relatively less exposed to the spray. Taking his cigarettes from the top pocket of his coat, he glances surreptitiously at Ivor, downwind of him.

Intercepting his look, Ivor spots the cigarettes. "You're not intending to smoke one of those bloody things now, are you?" he snaps.

"As a matter of fact I am," returns George with a touch of defiance. "I'll change places with you if that makes you happier"

Ivor is more than willing to oblige. Moving hand over hand, he and George swap seats while the boat shifts heavily under them. Within seconds of sitting down, however, and before he has even begun considering how he is to light a match, George finds himself engulfed by a surge of water drenching him as completely as if a bucket had been emptied on his head. Whilst he forlornly examines the sodden wreck of the cigarette drooping from his fingers, Ivor, sheltered from the deluge, grins exultantly around.

"We'll keep to a course inside the islands up ahead," the skipper says, wiping beads of water from his face. "That way we'll avoid the worst of the wind." He indicates to Denzil the heading he wants him to take.

"Aye, aye, skipper!" Denzil says, turning the wheel a few degrees to port.

By and by the sea seems to settle down a little. Whether this is due to the skipper's choice of course or because the wind is losing some of its strength is not certain. At any rate, with the buffeting from the waves decreasing, the boat now begins to make significantly better headway. Zack replaces Denzil at the helm while the skipper checks the speed.

"We're making between five and six knots," he announces. "Not bad in these conditions! I did think we were in for a good six hours' run when we left Rogoznica, but at this rate we'll be at Trogir within three hours."

"Suits me!" grunts Ivor. "Don't think I'm complaining, but that forecast of fifty knot winds was a bit off target, wasn't it? We haven't met with any gusts much above twenty-seven, as far as I can make out."

"The wind strength'll be stronger further out to sea," replies the skipper. "We'll be all right if we keep close inshore like this."

Despite their faster progress, the *Isabella* is still bouncing uncomfortably from one wave crest to the next. Gradually they encounter more and more boats heading in the opposite direction. Under full sail and with the wind behind them, they are scudding through the water like racing yachts. Their occupants, casual in shorts and tee-shirts, curiously survey our heroes with their raised hoods and jackets zipped up to their chins.

"'Ere, skipper, why can't we go the other way?" asks Denzil in an aggrieved tone. "It'd be one 'ell of a sight easier!"

After some time the weather, having seemed about to show its friendlier face, decides instead to fall into a sulk. The sky darkens, and the first raindrops the crew have seen all week begin to splatter the cockpit. They make little difference to those crewmen who are already soaked with spray, but the skipper thinks it wise to raise the bimini all the same. This proves no easy task, for the wind still has strength enough to hamper their efforts, but with Frank balanced on the coachroof wrestling the boom aside, and Zack and Ivor straining to secure the straps, the cover is at last in place.

As he tumbles back into the cockpit, Frank finds himself noticeably damper than before, but at least the bimini now offers shelter from the rain and the worst of the spray. With the sky growing ever blacker, thoughts of sailing in home waters inevitably spring to mind.

"We might just as well be in Scotland!" rumbles Stan, gazing out at the grey sea and sky.

"What, and miss all this fun!" squawks Denzil.

Arthur's thoughts are turning to his kettle. His seasickness pills have lulled him into a gentle doze over the past half hour, but now he is growing more wide awake he feels in need of some activity.

"Cup of tea, anyone?" he inquires.

All thankfully accept the offer, and he descends to the galley.

"Would I be right in thinkin', skipper," Stan bellows as Arthur disappears below, "as we'll not be needin' lunch on the run today?"

The skipper consults the time. "No," he replies. "We can eat when we get to Trogir. If we keep up this speed we'll be there within the hour."

A further set of course adjustments sees the *Isabella* entering more sheltered waters, and at last their destination comes into view through the rain, now turning to a steady drizzle.

On drawing nearer, all eyes are peeled for the fuel pontoon where they need to top up the diesel before returning the boat to the marina. As it turns out, the fuel pontoon does not take much locating. Off the starboard bow they spot a cluster of yachts circling or manoeuvring to hold station. Beyond these the fuel pump is plainly visible. Unfortunately, there is only room beside it for one boat at a time.

"Look at that queue! Now that's what I call good planning!" comments the skipper, taking over the helm from Zack and placing the *Isabella* as best he can at the edge of the waiting boats. It takes a good hour, with the skipper nudging the throttle back and forth to keep the *Isabella* more or less in place, before their turn at the pump arrives. But at the last moment, just as the skipper is beginning his approach, a boat comes racing from behind and, overtaking them, ties up and begins fuelling.

"I bet they're Germans!" mutters George. "They never wait their turn!"

There follows a good deal of grumbling among the crew about Germans and their disdain for orderly queuing. Some go even further, and are inclined to blame the entire German nation not only for this breach of etiquette, but also for the wind, the rain and all the other vicissitudes of their passage here.

At length, however, the offending boat pulls clear, and the *Isabella* takes its place at the pontoon.

"Vielen Dank!" bawls Denzil at the departing boat's stern, and is surprised to receive merely blank looks in response.

"Something tells me they weren't German!" observes Ivor.

"Well, you'd think they'd bloody understand that all the same," complains Denzil, preparing to jump ashore with a mooring line.

"I thought Bulic was supposed to be sending someone to meet us here," says Zack, addressing the skipper. "There's no sign of anyone!"

"That's what he told me," replies the skipper, watching Frank take the fuel line and pass it to Ivor on the boat. "Still, that's not much of a surprise. I can't think why he wanted us met here anyway. It's not as if we need assistance at this stage. I'm sure we can manage on our own now!"

"We've damn well 'ad to so far today!" bellows Stan.

Refuelling completed, they make for their appointed berth in the marina. The drizzle is still falling steadily as, for the last time, the skipper slides the boat into its mooring. Predictably, there is no trace of Mr. Bulic on the pontoon, but an underling from the charter company is in attendance to hand Ivor the lazy line. Having made the line secure, Ivor's first action on stepping ashore is to buttonhole this individual and pin him to the spot with his most assertive gaze.

"Look here!" he begins, folding his arms to make himself even more formidable than usual. "What the hell do you people mean by making us put to sea with a forecast of fifty knot winds and no life raft on board? That's not good, not good at all!"

Nervously the underling looks Ivor up and down. Towering over him and bristling with outrage, Ivor has the air of a malign and very angry walrus. Overawed, the underling attempts a feeble smile, raises both arms in a gesture of incomprehension, then turns briskly on his heels and beats a swift retreat.

"Don't you think you should have spoken to the organ grinder rather than the monkey?" the skipper asks as Ivor stomps back up the gangplank.

Ivor looses off a series of harumphs, then, his bristles falling back into place, breaks into a grin.

"Oh, but I did enjoy that!" he exclaims, beaming in all directions until his eye encounters George drawing on a cigarette next to the companionway. "Hey, Puffing Billy, you get that bloody smoke downwind of me!" he snaps, his grin fading instantly. And with that he settles down on the only dry spot left in the cockpit to enjoy the last of his special sweets in splendid isolation.

Thoughts now turn to lunch, and Stan sets to scouring the fridge for anything still edible. There will be no garlic bread today, supplies of garlic being at a low ebb. Stan himself is not greatly upset at this prospect.

"I'll not mind if I don't see another bit o' garlic bread for a long time!" He rumbles, extracting a lump of mouldy and malodorous cheese from the deeper recesses of the fridge. Dumping the cheese unceremoniously into the waste bin, he delves further into the fridge's underbelly like a pathologist conducting a post mortem. "It'd be a bloody good thing if we didn't 'ave to keep switchin' this fridge off when we're not usin' the engine! Things go mouldy too quick," he resonates with a ferocious sniff. He pushes a pack of orange juice aside. "'Ere!" he thunders, straightening up. "There's still some beer under all this lot!" This news instantly conveys itself to Frank, till now engaged in observing the comings and goings on the pontoon. In a flash Frank is at his side, and in another he is at the saloon table nursing a pack of beer cans, watching Arthur put together salami sandwiches from ingredients already salvaged by Stan.

Lunch is a scratch affair, its general purpose being to see off whatever remains of the provisions. The crew apply themselves to this task with a will. Both food and beer vanish in the twinkling of an eye. In the end only a few meagre dregs of wine and two or three bottles containing spirits still remain.

"Looks as if the weather's getting better," remarks Frank, seeing his empty beer can catch a glint of sunshine from the hatch overhead.

"Yes," agrees the skipper. "The rain seems to have stopped. We might be in for a pleasant afternoon in spite of everything!"

He proves right. In the afternoon the sun does indeed make an appearance, the clouds disperse and all the morning's discomforts are forgotten. In groups of two or three the crew set off to explore the bars and cafes of the town. When, eventually, they drift back they haul out their bags and set about packing in a desultory fashion to be ready for tomorrow's taxi ride to the airport.

"It'll be long trousers in the morning," says the skipper regretfully, tossing a pair of shorts into his bag. "No more short trousers for a while! It is September, after all!"

"Too right, mate!" replies Denzil, taking one green and one red sock from his own bag and holding them up for inspection. "It's a funny thing, but I've got another pair just like this back 'ome!" He slips off his shoes and tries the socks on for effect. "Port an' starboard, eh? What d'you think o' that?"

Ivor's head protrudes from the forepeak doorway. "You've got those on the wrong feet!" he growls.

"They're the only ones I've got!" retorts Denzil, examining his lower extremities to make sure.

Out of all the crew only Zack seems noticeably tense. It appears that, having twice searched exhaustively through both cockpit lockers, he cannot find his flippers. He scours the boat, growing ever more frustrated in the process, and loosing off enough uniquely colourful expletives to make even the saltiest sea-dog reach for a dictionary.

Finally he goes up on deck, where, after stamping about for a full five minutes above the others' heads, he comes upon the missing items dangling from the anchor at the bow. Stalking back, he descends to the saloon and aims an accusing look first at George's closed cabin door, then at Denzil bent over his bag. Paying no attention, Denzil launches into a rendition of 'Be kind to your web-footed friends' whilst pressing his knee hard down on the bag. With a scowl, Zack disappears into his cabin to resume his interrupted packing.

The approach of evening brings with it the last rounds of drinks in the cockpit. Now the crew's task is to consume the remainder of the spirits. This is a serious business. An inventory is taken. It seems there is gin left, but very little tonic. There is also Irish whiskey which Ivor has thus far kept to himself, and there are rumours of a bottle of brandy which, along with Denzil, has for the moment vanished without trace. In the fullness of time both Denzil and the brandy do in fact reappear, the latter visibly reduced in volume. Among the remainder of the crew, by now experimenting with novel admixtures of gin and dry ginger, his re-emergence goes unnoticed. It is only when, having cleared away the glasses and empty bottles, they go ashore for dinner, that the full extent of Denzil's private indulgence starts to grow apparent.

It should be noted that, in spite of his travails with local place-names, Denzil has always reckoned himself something of a linguist. Not only has he made inroads into night-school German, but he has also made it a practice, following trips abroad, to learn at least some rudiments of the language of whatever country he last visited. Over time this practice has added Spanish to his repertoire, and has brought him to a habit of launching willy-nilly into any language that seems appropriate as often as he can, a habit growing more persistent in direct proportion to his level of inebriation.

This evening, as he enters the restaurant selected earlier by Stan, Denzil's ear catches the distinctive strains of a Nordic language rising from a nearby table. As if propelled by an irresistible force he makes a beeline for this table and, grinning genially, hails the group seated there in a slurred accent: "Guten Abend, meine Herren! Wo kommen Sie her?"

The awkward silence that initially ensues has little impact on him. Even the eventual response, in perfect English: "We are actually from Copenhagen. We are Danish, not German!" makes scarcely any more impression.

"Entschuldigen Sie, bitte!" he responds with a wave and a cheery smile, before teetering to the next table where a Dutch family are quietly enjoying their dinner. "Guten Abend!" he begins again, but is luckily distracted at this point by a waiter manoeuvring a tray of brimming beer glasses past him.

"Just a mo' there, me old cocker!" he addresses the waiter, reverting automatically to his own vernacular. "We'll 'ave a few o' they when you're ready!"

His ear not quite attuned to Denzil's accent, the waiter passes on, leaving Denzil to meander haphazardly towards the table where skipper and crew are now perusing the menu.

"I've ordered drinks!" he announces, collapsing onto an empty chair between Ivor and Zack, both of whom shift their seats to one side.

The skipper hands him a menu. After attempting first to decipher this upside down, Denzil discovers his error, turns the menu the right way up and, after some indecision, settles on the lobster. He then sinks into a state of quiescence, toying absently with his cutlery until the waiter arrives to take the order.

"'Oy, mate, where's me beer?" he pipes up, only to be silenced by a dig in the ribs from Ivor, who until now has been doing his best to ignore him altogether. Having enlivened a degree or so, Denzil now applies himself to tutoring the waiter in the art of appending to each utterance the phrase 'me old cocker'. A quick learner, the waiter proves remarkably adept at this, and some minutes later can be heard presenting a bottle of Sauvignon Blanc to an elderly British couple some tables away with the words: "Your wine, me old cocker!" Though the couple smile politely back at him, they cast a highly disapproving look at Denzil.

The lobster, occupying the whole of Denzil's attention throughout the meal, proves a happy choice. Only occasionally when a piece of flesh, inexpertly detached, flies from his fork to make an unscheduled landing on a neighbouring table does he draw unwelcome attention to himself. On each of these occasions Ivor frowns, his eyes focusing on some vague point in the middle distance as he mentally absents himself from his surroundings.

"I thought bloody Ironbladder was bad enough!" he mutters under his breath, glancing quickly at

Frank whose glazed and vacant stare reflects his own serene detachment from reality.

Surprisingly, by the meal's end Denzil seems to have sobered up a little. As the crew rise to leave he advances on the waiter, shakes him warmly by the hand and apologises for his earlier rumbustiousness.

"Is not problem, me old cocker!" replies the waiter with a dismissive flourish of his hand.

Shepherding Denzil between them, the crew make their way back to the boat, Ivor walking in the lead to avoid further embarrassment en route.

"Well skipper," says George as they tramp up the gangplank and settle in the cockpit to extract the very last drops of liquid from the very last bottle of gin, "this may have been a trip to remember, but it's not been all bad!"

"No, that's true," agree the others. Even Ivor, after first ascertaining that George is not in the process of lighting up, adds his voice to the chorus.

"We may have had our ups and downs," he observes, with the air of a professor concluding a lecture, "but on the whole it's been enjoyable enough. There's nothing like good company, I say!"

"You ain't wrong there, me old cocker!" asserts Denzil, slapping him vigorously on the back. "And you lot 'ave been nothing like good company!" He titters so appreciatiovely at his own joke that he gives himself a fit of hiccups.

Despite Ivor's watchfulness, George has succeeded in lighting a furtive cigarette. He inhales deeply and puffs forth a haze of smoke that sends Ivor into a paroxysm of coughing.

"It's a bloody good job we all get on so well, or I don't know 'ow we'd manage!" thunders Stan, knocking back the few remaining droplets of gin.

The moment has come for the skipper to round things off. "Well, lads, are we up for another trip next year?" he queries.

"Why not?" the crew respond as one.

"Yeah, why not?" echoes Denzil between hiccups. "After all, I've 'eard said, worse things 'appen ashore!"

"Anyone for tea?" asks Arthur.

THE LESSON BEING - DON'T GO
SAILING WITH OLD FARTS !